THE UGLY TRUTH

ARON BEAUREGARD

JOHN SKIPP

SHANE McKENZIE

WARNING:
This book contains scenes and subject matter that are
disgusting and disturbing; easily offended people are not the
intended audience.

FOR EXCLUSIVE OFFERS AND UPDATES JOIN
OUR MAILING LISTS AT:

Aron Beauregard: substack.com/@abhorror

John Skipp: substack.com/@yerpalskipp

Shane McKenzie: substack.com/@shanemckenziehorror

FOR SIGNED BOOKS, MERCHANDISE, AND
EXCLUSIVE ITEMS VISIT:

Aron Beauregard: www.ABHorror.com

Shane McKenzie: www. McHorror.net

For Kristopher Triana, Bear, & Shadow.

"A harmful truth is better than a useful lie."

–Thomas Mann

PART 1:

MAKING GOOD

BY ARON BEAUREGARD

THE HARDEST PART IS SHOWING UP

I never understood the pain I'd caused until I felt it for myself. As I sat listening nervously to the guru of going straight, Royce O'Riley, I finally knew that I was ready to commit to changing. Which is *exactly* why I felt so nervous.

"You've got to live it like you mean it!" Royce yelled, punching the air in front of him.

The intensity in his eyes felt like it was transferring into my soul. The voids inside me that I'd ponied up the $399 to address seemed more possible to fill.

Attending this seminar is the best decision I've ever made, I thought.

"But I can't do it for you—I wish I could ... but I can't," Royce continued. "Every man has his day. And once you're committed to letting go of the lies, to breaking the habits, you'll encounter that moment of clarity. If it's happening for you now, then you see them already. You see their frowning faces. Just close your eyes and I promise they'll appear—everyone your lies and deceptions have destroyed."

I didn't want to close my eyes—I'd seen their faces many times before. They'd been haunting me since my revelation.

"And now ... it's time to get to work." The grin of enthusiasm slowly melted off Royce's face as he directed his gaze toward the woman sitting at the check-in table by the door of the hotel conference room. "Thanks again, everyone, for coming. It's cash or card on the way out, please. *No* checks."

A thunderous applause rattled the room as some of the people began to file out toward the table. A handful of other folks made their way up to Royce to shake his hand and commend him for his talk. I waited, knowing that I needed more than a handshake.

As the line dwindled, I rushed to the podium, hellbent on catching him before he exited.

"Excuse me, Mr. O'Riley," I said.

He lifted a briefcase before locking eyes with me.

"Yeah?"

"If I may, I just have one question."

Royce furrowed his brow, seeming slightly annoyed. "I suppose, if it's just one."

"What exactly did you mean when you said it's time to get to work? I think I know ... but I just need to be sure."

"What do *you* think I meant?"

"That it's time for us to make amends with those faces we see."

He grinned and patted the side of my shoulder. "Don't ever let anyone tell you you're not a good listener."

As he was about to turn and head for the door, I knew it was now or never.

"But what if the things I've done are ... irreversible?" I asked.

The question caused Royce's stride to freeze—something I said must've caught his attention. "Then ... you might have to get creative. You might have to find a way to admit to yourself that your journey isn't about what you think it is."

I didn't have time for riddles. Every morning I awoke, I did so on the edge of a cliff. One sunrise, I was bound to fall off of it.

"But what does that mean?" I begged.

Royce chuckled to himself. "What's your name, friend?"

"Howard—Howard Oates," I said. "But my friends call me Howie."

Every second he paused, I waited anxiously, anticipating. I needed someone to tell me what to do, but there was no one left. I needed to find a way to address the spiderweb of horror that I'd spun.

"You're already living it like you mean it, Howard—and that's the most important step. But what I'm trying to say is sometimes the path to atonement can only be carved out by sacrifice. Sometimes the sacrifice is indirect, and sometimes it's personal. But you can't comprehend the cost of your actions until you've calculated the price of *all* the ramifications."

I tried to put everything he was saying together in my head, absorbing each word of wisdom the man was willing to offer me. I could feel the sweat starting to bead at the crown of my skull, knowing that if I followed his advice, I'd be opening up Pandora's Box.

"Now you'll have to excuse me," Royce said, handing me a business card. "I know you can do it. If you require additional guidance, my website has more books to help you."

As I took the info from him, Royce nodded.

"Card only, though," he said. "*No* checks."

"Thank you," I whispered.

After Royce disappeared through the rear exit of the conference room, I made my way up to the table and paid for my session. I slipped out the automatic doors and into the cold, immediately lighting a cigarette. Once I made it to my car, I turned it on, hoping the heat would get that nip off the back of my neck.

I slipped Royce's card into the hardcover copy of *The Lies We Lay*—his first and most popular book. While I appreciated the gesture of the card and additional details he was offering for a nominal fee, for the first time, I felt like I knew everything I needed to. I felt like it was now just a matter of forcing myself to do what I knew I had to.

I tossed the box of menthol Dart's on the seat next to the hardcover and looked through the windshield.

Wherever I look, it's always there.

I shook my head as I stared at the remnants of an icy snowbank in front of my parking space.

You'll never escape it.

I don't know why I never moved on from the brutal cold of the Northeast. I hate it. The simplest answer is probably because I didn't cultivate any sort of professional experience or career that could reap enough funds to rescue me from it.

All the ruthless winter weather did was stir up horrible memories. As I took another drag of the cool menthol, I watched the red cherry on the tip of the Dart flare up in the rearview, unable to stop my mind from wandering back to those dreadful times.

CAUSE AND EFFECT

As the smoke filled my virgin lungs, I started to violently cough. The burning sensation deep in my body hit as my eyes glossed over.

"First time's always a little harsh," Dad said, plucking the cigarette from my fingers and taking a drag for himself.

I eyed the cup of water next to Dad's pack of menthol Darts on the floor. As my coughing fit started to subside, I grabbed it from the collection of surrounding junk and took a drink. It was only after taking a sip, when I set the cup down, that I noticed there were flakes of ashes and a stale, extinguished cigarette butt floating in the water.

The gritty flakes of residue stuck to my tongue as an earthy taste resonated inside my mouth. I winced.

"My throat s-still hurts," I said.

Dad brushed it off like he did whenever I complained about anything. "Well, you're the one who said you were cold, right? These'll warm you up."

As I looked around the dark apartment, the mounds of garbage and filth gave me a feeling of claustrophobia. It felt like they were closing in on me. The lack of light made the sounds of the vermin living alongside us unsettling.

I coughed again, the conditions so frigid that my cloud of exhale hung in the air several seconds before dissolving.

"I d-don't feel any warmer," I said, shivering in my jacket.

"Of course you don't. One puff isn't going to fucking change anything."

"But I don't think I can smoke anymore—it makes me feel sick. Can't w-we just turn the heat on?"

"I wish it was that simple, Son—I really do." Dad turned and looked at me, putting his hand on my back. "But your mother's out there working hard. She's bringing something home that'll warm us all up. I'm telling you, this stuff makes the cold not even matter. It lights a fire inside you. It'll fix everything, always does." He raised the butt and glared at it. "Much better than these things."

"You p-p-promise?"

"I promise. But you've gotta be brave enough to take it. It's usually only for adults ... but I think you're mature for your age." Dad squinted at me, racking his brain. "How old are you now?"

He asked the question like he was joking with me, but I could see in his eyes that my age was probably a mystery to him.

I laughed, doing my best to make light of it. "I'll be eight in two months."

The rotten teeth forming his grin were slowly covered up by his cracked lips.

"What's wrong?" I asked.

For a moment, it seemed like he wasn't even there. It was like when he gazed into the stained wall of the bedroom, he was looking past it.

"Nothing ..." he whispered. "Sure does go by fast."

Our conversation was interrupted by a pounding on the door. Dad's eyes widened as he reached for the baseball bat on the side of the dirty mattress lying on the floor.

"Wait here," he said, tossing the butt into the cup.

I looked out the doorway, watching him approach the front door, readying the bat.

"Who the fuck is it?" Dad asked.

I could hear Mom's muffled voice. "It's me. Open the goddamn door—it's freezing out here."

Dad quickly undid the locks and chain latch on the door, and just as soon as Mom slipped inside, he resecured it.

"Did you get it?" The stress in Dad's tone was intense. "Did you?!"

"Yeah, yeah," Mom snarled.

"Well, let me see it!" Dad begged.

"I'm the one who stole it, so I'm going first."

"What do you mean? If I hadn't cooked up a story for you to feed Jesse and told you where he kept his shit, you wouldn't have nothing!"

My mother glared at him, the rage and eagerness battling inside her pupils. "Don't be a dick, Sam. There's plenty for both of us."

Mom rushed into the room, extracted the tan ball from her jacket, and plopped onto the floor. She started to sift through the pile of trash until she located a blackened spoon and needle.

I'd seen her and Dad shoot up many times before. Nothing about their manic process made me want to do what they did.

Not the sharp point of the rusty needle.

Not the powder mutating into the dirty liquid.

Not their eyes sunsetting or the strange babblings they emitted as the drug took hold of them.

But I was so fucking cold. I didn't know any better. I only knew what they'd taught me. In that moment of pure desperation, the junk in that needle was the closest my family could get to warmth.

As Mom lay back on a heap of stained clothing and nodded off, Dad yanked the spike out of her bloody arm.

When my nerves got to me and I started crying, Dad did his best to comfort me.

"There's nothing to be scared of, buddy. I'm not gonna give you as much as Mom took. Just enough to warm you up. You trust me, don't you?"

My crying morphed into a rapid stutter of sniffles. "Y-y-yeah, Dad. I-I do."

"Then just roll up your little sleeve and relax." He used his dirty fingers to wipe Mom's fluid off the shaft of the needle and cooked up a small shot for me. "It's just a little blood, nothing to worry about. It's just like when you went to the doctor's office when you were younger—no different. This is just medicine. And what does medicine do?"

"W-what?"

He smiled kindly. "It makes you all better."

As his rotten grin closed in on me, I turned away from my arm and closed my eyes. I wiped away the chilly wetness on my lashes and waited for the warmth.

"Just a little pinch ..." Dad whispered, "until you feel like a prince."

The poke only lasted a second, but I felt it deeper than I expected to.

"All done," Dad whispered.

The words sounded like they were oozing out of his mouth like sludge from a sewer pipe. My heart started to race as panic gripped me. But as the beats ramped up, a sudden wave of calm cascaded over me, followed by a surge of what I can only call pure euphoria. I wanted to open my eyes, but my lids didn't seem to budge. And suddenly, the nasty things were gone.

I couldn't smell the funk in the bedroom.

I couldn't feel the cold penetrating my body to the bone.

I wasn't thinking about how my life always felt like one big disaster that was continuing to unfold.

It was when I felt myself smiling that my eyelids finally came open. Dad held the needle between his teeth while the flame now sat at the bottom of an even bigger spoon.

"Mom got hers," Dad mumbled to himself. "And little Howie got his." As he dipped the needle into the utensil, the glass barrel filled up to capacity—loaded with more than double the smack my mother had injected. "So ... I guess it's only right that Dad gets his."

The pile of uncomfortable trash against my back was no longer poking and prodding me. I felt like I was lying on a cloud. I could hear myself groaning and the ticking of my heart inside my ears.

As the fluid disappeared into my dad's arm, I felt excited. Soon, he would feel just as good as I did. Even when I watched his body seize up and him slump onto his side, I still felt the warm blissful feeling fizzing inside my torso. Even when his jaw unhinged and the foamy saliva started to discharge from it, I felt better than ever.

It's like when I used to blow bubbles in the backyard during the summer, I thought. *It looks so fun.*

Even when it felt like hours had gone by without Dad blinking, I remained happy. So, *so* happy.

PERSPECTIVE

The car had finally warmed up, but as I stared out into the dark street, I knew it wasn't the same warmth I'd felt that night when I was eight years old. As I put the car in reverse and headed home, I couldn't help but play through the rest of it. The twists and turns that occurred in my life were all I had left to ponder anymore. There was nothing left to distract me from the rotten retreads.

I lit up another Dart after snubbing out the last one in the ashtray. It was strange knowing that my first cigarette was also my dad's last. I wonder if that was why I stuck to smoking—in a weird way, it comforted me. Then, on the other hand, while the temptation of smack always loomed in the back of my mind, I'd never fallen back on it.

Even after all the shit you've been through, I thought. *That's a fucking miracle in itself.*

When I'd watched Dad die, I'd felt like a million bucks. And even later that night, when our front door got kicked in, I wasn't scared. Even when I watched Jesse—the guy my mom had ripped off—put the knife to her throat and ask her where the shit was, I still felt invincible.

What a feeling.

And even when Jesse put together that all his dope had already found veins and he used that corroded blade to cut open her throat and expose the deep red meat underneath, my mood remained joyous.

I remember him looking down on me, into my dilated pupils—not angry like he had looked down at my dad's corpse or my mother as she gurgled and bled out. When he looked down at me, he was sad.

I still don't know why.

As I turned down the one-way, I bit my lip. When I got to thinking about this stuff, I bit it so hard that I drew blood from time to time.

That's when it started.

The lying was essentially a genetic trait for a kid with junkie parents. They lied to everyone. They lied to each other. It was the lying and storytelling that got them killed.

With my folks gone, I got rehomed with my Aunt Abbie. Unlike my mess of a father, she was a quiet woman who was completely straight. Still, in my time living with her, our relationship was very transactional. I never felt the warmth with her. And while I appreciate Aunt Abbie bringing a sense of stability to my life, I could tell she was just doing her part because it was the right thing to do, not because she felt bad for me or actually wanted to.

As I pulled into the apartment complex and searched for a parking space, I recalled what that strange phase of my life was like. A boy dragged through years of trauma, with no one else in the world to relate to. Facing his polite but detached aunt each evening at the dinner table.

That's when the lying started.

How in God's name could I *not* fucking lie? I mean, what was I supposed to tell the other kids when they asked about my parents? Should I tell them my junkie dad shot me up with smack before his fatal dose? Should I talk about watching my prostitute mother's neck get sawed open? It was easier to tell them that they were cruise ship entertainers or in the military. Anything was better than the truth. *Anything.*

But as I grew older, I started to resent all the falsehoods I'd spread. I felt like a fidgety street dweller trying to swindle his next fix. But the fix I was in search of wasn't dope, or smoke, or crack.

It was acceptance.

It was after I grabbed Royce O'Riley's book, got out of the car, and approached the door to my apartment that I fell back into that period of time for a moment—when I'd still had a chance to do right. Before I'd seen any of their faces when I closed my eyes. When I'd decided to go cold turkey.

By the time I'd finished high school, I was ready to start fresh. All my "friends" at that point were superficial anyway, so it wasn't really too hard. And it's not that I was planning on becoming an open book or willingly spouting my history to every stranger in my immediate circumference. I'd just committed to saying less and staying honest. But when I'd made the decision to leave what my parents had taught me behind and to go out into the real world as a real person, I thought I was leaving my roots of deceit behind for good.

But if one thing's been true in my life, it's that my past has always had a way of circling back.

THE FACES

I'd have given anything for another family day. As I set my keys and wallet down on the table, I looked at our photo on the wall. We were all so happy.

My wife, Farrah, had a grin as bright as pearls. I sat with my arm around her as she held Missy in a blanket.

Her little baby socks, I thought. *They were the cutest.*

Missy was less than a month into this world when the photo was taken. To our right sat our sweet son, Owen, brandishing the same beaming smile as his mother.

I just wanted them to have what I didn't. I wanted them to feel the warmth.

It was the lies that destroyed my family. And while they were lies that I believed were all justified—a necessity to protect them—knowing that now didn't fix it. Every time I looked at the picture, it pained me.

I diverted my attention to the book in my hand. I didn't need to read it—I'd done that three times already. But I did need to think about what Royce had said. I needed to figure out what my first move was going to be. I moseyed into the living room, plopped down on the recliner, and promptly lit a cigarette.

You can't comprehend the cost of your actions until you've calculated the price of all the ramifications.

After replaying Royce's words in my head, I took a puff and saw his face: Kevin Fargas. The sleazy car salesman's confident and reassuring cadence was burned into my mind, accompanied by the loud ticking of the engine. Just thinking about him made my skin crawl, but I couldn't stop there.

I had to listen to Royce.

With another drag of smoke came the haunting hack of Charlie Martindale as he cleared phlegm from his throat and spat out the window of his cab. I pictured myself in the back seat, watching him smugly take a slurp out of his coffee mug. I could practically smell the alcohol on his stinking breath, poorly camouflaged by cheap cologne.

Shaking my head, I didn't want to move on. The last face was the one I feared the most.

Gotta face all of them if I'm gonna make good.

Preparing myself, I took a drag so deep that the butt nearly burned down to the filter. When I saw Addison Wood's smooth face and the absolute dread in her eyes, I nearly teared up. No matter how many days passed, that was the one that still haunted me—she would forever be the one who haunted me.

I ... I can't start there.

Removing another Dart from the pack, I continued to chain smoke. Just thinking about what I was about to do was stressing me to the max. But I had to do it. I could either stay in that apartment alone and slowly lose my mind, or I could do what I had to. Despite being the honorable choice, in a way, it was still almost a selfish one.

Are you doing this for them? The three faces flickered in my brain again. *Or for yourself?*

Until that moment, I hadn't really considered the notion. But regardless of my subliminal motives or lack thereof, one thing remained true: it had to be done. In picturing the three of them, I felt like I'd come to the most logical conclusion. I had to start at the beginning.

Chronological order made the most sense. If I started with Addison, it might take such a toll on me that I might not get to Kevin or Charlie. Starting out low on the totem pole was the most logical approach. It gave me the best opportunity to make good on all of them.

The only problem was I had no idea how to begin. Pulling more smoke deep inside my lungs, I nervously scratched the side of my face. Looking at the computer sitting atop my desk in the corner of the room, I exhaled.

I guess that's as good a lead as any.

NASTY
NEIGHBORHOOD

Growing old is a privilege—a privilege that some of us will never see. But Jeanie Fargas had made the cut. After several hours of scouring the internet, I'd done what I needed to: tracked down the lone remaining relative of Kevin Fargas.

His mother now resided in a home for the elderly that looked a little rough around the edges. The pictures on the internet usually made those places look better than they actually were. But it seemed the good people at Ridgeway Retirement Home hadn't gone out of their way to disguise the property's warts. Between the dirty aesthetic and the crumbling walls, and the photos of the building's disgruntled inhabitants, the place seemed a mess. And as my car pulled closer to the address, it was clear that the neighborhood it resided in was every bit as nasty as the building itself.

A pair of bums screamed in a rage as I rolled past them. It wasn't clear what they were upset about. They were probably just upset that they were stuck in such a place, desperately looking for any way out.

This is it, I thought, pulling into the facility's parking lot.

I found a spot in the back, tucking myself away from the vagrants. I needed to have a smoke before I went through with my plan. If the street dwellers had me in their line of sight, I knew they would at the very least pester me for a cigarette. But tucked away under a tree with one side of the car flanked by a snowbank and the other by a van, I hoped they would overlook my presence.

"I ... I can't fucking do this," I mumbled to myself, squirming in my seat.

As I reconsidered my reasoning, I couldn't help but think about the string of events that led me to that very parking lot—to teetering on the cusp of meeting Kevin Fargas's geriatric mother. I didn't want to go down that road again. I'd been down it too many times before. But as I tried to convince myself to back down, I knew reliving it was the only thing that might motivate me.

I put the cigarette to my lips and closed my eyes.

THE LEMON

The interior of the car was cherry. Despite being a used vehicle, it still had that new car smell. As I drove down the snowy road, I couldn't help but admire the country beauty. The dusting on the pines made everything around us seem so clean. A far cry from the polluted snow we dealt with all winter in the city.

I remember the wide grin on Kevin Fargas's face when he'd sold me the SUV. How he'd tried to gas me up when I was debating signing the paperwork.

"Sure, it's an older vehicle, but with this kind of milage, you could drive this fuckin' thing off the lot today and across the goddamn country. You said you want something that can take the family on a trip, right? Well, then look no further. This baby even has snow tires."

I couldn't believe we were actually doing it. For the first time, I was doing what real families do—I was treating my kids to the life I never had. With any luck, Farrah would be impressed by the remote cabin I'd rented, and we might even have a little intimate time while the kids were asleep.

"Owen, honey," Farrah said, "can you grab me another blanket from the back?"

"Sure, Mom," Owen said.

She draped a second blanket over her lap, still shivering as she looked out at the ice-capped body of water.

I put my hand on her thigh. "You okay, babe?"

"Yeah, just a little cold," she said. "I think my Crohn's is flaring up again."

"I can crank the heat if you want."

She shook her head. "I don't want Missy getting too warm. I'll just bundle up. Owen, can you check on your sister?"

The boy glanced at the backward car seat before putting his finger to his lips and politely shushing his mother. "She's still sleeping."

"Okay, well, we're almost there," I said. "It shouldn't be more than another forty-five minutes. Sorry, the forecast didn't say anything about more snow."

"I'll be fine." Farrah grinned, excitedly taking in scenery. "I'm just excited for our first vacation."

"Can you believe it? A remote cabin retreat, just the four of us. No loud horns honking, no light pollution, and, most importantly, no people."

"I'm definitely getting the sense of isolation. Feels like we haven't seen another car in forever ... This place is really out there."

"I can't wait to see it," Owen chimed in.

I winked at him in the rearview. "Won't be long now, bud."

When I'd left the turbulence of high school behind and entered the real world, I never imagined I could achieve such normalcy. Farrah and I had started out as work friends. But after many hangouts and realizing how much we had in common, we both kind of sensed that it would be a crime if we didn't take it to the next level.

It happened slow, and I think that's why I was finally able to open up to her. And when I did, for the first time, she gave me faith in society. Farrah had accepted me—she was the lone person I'd been able to share the dark bits of my past with. It felt like she'd ripped the monkey off my back.

Our conversations were therapeutic. When I revealed what my parents were like and how things ended for them, she sympathized and listened. Even after I told her about the façade I'd created for myself in high school and how I'd constantly lied to everyone, desperately trying to create any semblance of normalcy, Farrah never judged me.

I could tell it hurt her to learn my secrets, but she didn't use that discomfort as an excuse to look down on me. She told me that I was strong. She commended me for transcending the horror and finding a way to deal with my demons.

It was Farrah who wanted to have a family. I was hesitant at first. I didn't know what kind of parent I would be. The idea frightened me. If I had a child, would I suddenly pivot onto the path my father went down?

You know exactly what not *to do,* I recalled her saying. *You'll be wonderful. I know you will, Howie.*

She was right. If I hadn't met Farrah, I might've been a slave to that irrational fear for my entire life. But it went so well after we had Owen. So well that it was *my* idea to have a second child.

As I continued down the snowy road, I truly felt like I was in a winter wonderland. The cold would always bring back terrible memories of my childhood, but it was so much easier to bear with the support of my family. They gave me the strength and drive to do anything.

"What's that noise?" Farrah asked.

The loud snap that came from under the hood was followed by several subtle ticks and pings. The noises from the engine block quickly transitioned into a series of loud knocks.

"What the hell?" I said.

Feeling the power drain out of the vehicle, I veered off the road just as the SUV died.

"Oh, my God," Farrah said. "This isn't happening."

"What's wrong?" Owen asked.

I felt dread blossoming inside my belly but tried to keep everyone calm. "It's gonna be okay. Whatever it is, I'm sure it's just a minor setback."

"We—we just bought this goddamn car," Farrah said, growing visibly upset.

As Missy awoke and started to cry, I could see the concern on Owen's face in the rearview. His mother never cussed, so her choice of language in itself would've been a red flag. And when I tried restarting the car, to no avail, it couldn't have deterred his worry any.

"We're fine, just everybody relax. I'll figure it out," I reassured them, popping the hood. I turned to Farrah. "Let me just have a quick look and I'll be right back."

"Okay," Farrah whispered, looking at Owen. "Try to keep your sister calm."

I rushed out of the car and got under the hood. The frayed timing belt couldn't have been more obvious.

"Fuck!" I yelled. "How?"

It didn't make sense. The milage on the SUV was low. It wasn't due for a timing belt change for a long time. I forced my anger aside, slowly coming to grips with the realization that on this lonely stretch of road, in the middle of a snowstorm, we were now in a survival situation. Fishing around in my jacket, I whipped out my phone. I can't say I was surprised to see no bars on the screen, but I was still horrified. Still, it wasn't a difficult decision. There was only one option.

Shuffling to the passenger side of the car, I waved Farrah out. As she reluctantly exited the vehicle, I could see the worry on her face compounding in real time. And with her hand clasped over her belly, I could see her Crohn's flare-up wasn't being helped by the situation. She shivered as I pulled her in for a hug.

"What's wrong?" she asked.

Hearing the crack in her voice broke my heart. And watching Owen nervously try his best to comfort Missy in the backseat ripped it in half.

"I'm gonna try and make a run for that gas station a few miles back," I finally said.

"A few miles back?! That was, like, ten miles! It's freezing out, just—just call someone!"

"There's no service, Farrah. It's the only way. I'll go, and you stay with the kids and keep an eye out for any cars."

She broke down, sobbing hysterically. "W-w-what if no one comes? W-what if you don't get back in—"

I hugged her tight. The cold had found me again. Suddenly, I felt like that lost little boy freezing on the bedroom floor of the dope house. As I looked at Owen again, I came to grips with what I had done. Inadvertently or not, in that moment, looking at my little boy was like staring into a mirror that projected my past.

You've got to fix it, I thought.

"I promise you," I whispered. "I'll be back."

***

Fargas Motor's was a place I never imagined stepping foot inside again, never mind breaking into. But with Kevin all by his lonesome, as that piece of shit rambled on the phone, I'd heard all I needed to validate my presence.

"You're my goddamn mechanic," Kevin said. "I tell you what to do and when to do it. So tomorrow, work the Honda, understood?" There was a brief pause. "Right. Did you fish that odometer outta the totaled Cavalier and swap it yet? I need that fuckin' car ready to sell. It's been taking up lot space."

My suspicion had proven true: that timing belt didn't snap randomly—that piece of shit scammed me. Suddenly, my brain sparked.

That two-faced piece of shit. Every goddamn word he told me about that car was a lie.

As I toyed with the pair of handcuffs, even through my black gloves, I could feel the cold steel. When I'd happened upon the cuffs at an antique store, I felt sick. The moment I'd seen them, it was like they were calling to me. It didn't strike me until much later why I'd even purchased them.

Farrah and I used to love the nostalgia of antique stores. Not that we bought a ton of things, but even just looking was something we found joy in together.

She'd be glad you bought these.

She'd only been gone about a month, but it already felt like an eternity. After her funeral, I was a changed man. I couldn't stop thinking about those wrong turns I took backtracking to the gas station during the whiteout. I couldn't help but blame myself. When I looked at her lips during the wake, I could still see some blue under the layers of makeup.

With Farrah battling Crohn's, the coroner surmised that her anemic state was ultimately what caused her to freeze to death. And while Owen and Missy were both very sick as a result of being stranded in the storm, my lone silver lining was their survival.

Listening to those kids cry for weeks beat me down. And as I stared at Kevin through the holes in my ski mask, I wanted to open the closet door more than just a crack. After hearing the phone call, I could stop lying to myself. It wasn't my fault. It was that cocksucker's.

I pulled the handgun from the back of my waistband—my first investment after Farrah's death—and set my sights on one of the steel pillars that held up the frame of the garage. Being a single dad with two kids, I was currently pretty strapped for cash. But forking over the money for the pistol was a necessary evil. I'd never shot a gun before or even gotten into a fight. But I'd watched enough videos and felt like I was prepared to do whatever needed to be done. Even though I couldn't be certain that I was truly ready, I was prepared to find out.

When I burst out of the closet and leveled the barrel at him, shock rattled in his eyes.

"I've got money," Kevin cried. "Take whatever you—"

"I don't want your goddamn money," I said, tossing the handcuffs at him. I pointed to the steel pillar in the center of the room. "Put one of them on, then put your back to the beam."

"What the fuck is this?" Kevin asked. "Y-you want a car?"

"Actually, I do." Thrusting the gun toward him, I gritted my teeth. "Now put the fucking cuff on."

"O-okay! Okay!" Kevin clasped one around his left wrist and went to tighten the other.

"I said just one!"

"I'm cool," he said, putting his hands up.

"Back against the post."

Kevin did as I told him, and I fastened the other cuff tight. His arms were now behind his back, securing him to the pillar.

"What car do you want?" Kevin asked. "You can walk out of here right now with whatever you need! Just don't fucking kill me, man."

Watching the sweat pour off his face brought a smile to mine. His combover looked greasy as any I'd ever seen.

"Where's the Cavalier—the one you just swapped out the odometer in?"

He didn't acknowledge his wrongdoing, just nodded toward the bay. "It's out back, through the door. The switch is on the wall. Keys should be inside it."

I slipped the gun into my jacket and flipped the switch. When the door came open, I could see the bronze Cavalier just a few yards away. And when I got inside the car and turned the key, I realized Kevin was finally telling the truth for once.

Too little, too late.

My gloves gripped the steering wheel firm, and I pulled the car inside the building. When I slowed to a stop several feet away from Kevin, I could see he was *really* starting to sweat now.

Something about how everything had come together just made sense. When I bought the gun, I knew I wasn't going to use it on him. That wasn't me. Part of me wanted to get out of the car and give him a long-winded speech explaining why what was about to happen to him was going to happen. But that wasn't me either.

The car feels right.

As I revved the engine and glared at him, I saw piss start to bleed through the front of Kevin's khakis. He was screaming and yelling, but I wasn't listening. I'd cased his habits long enough to know no one was going to come to his aid.

No one was there to rescue my family when my children watched their mother cry herself to sleep. Why should it be any different for you?

At first, I didn't know if I could do it. But it was almost like my body made the decision for me. Suddenly, the car was in drive and the bumper was smashing into Kevin's thighs. The shrill sound of his screeches echoed as I put the car in reverse and rolled it back.

With his legs no longer pinned to the metal, they folded under the weight of his hefty frame. Sliding to the ground with his broken legs bent awkwardly, I could see the blood starting to pool. The sharp end of one of his thigh bones had found daylight. From the position he was in, that big oily head of his was aligned perfectly with the bumper.

He's fucking lucky. This is quicker than he deserves.

When I pressed the gas, I could feel the car applying pressure to his cranium. The cracking resounded like a chorus of people taking a bite out of an apple at the same time.

After I backed up a second time, I could see his head was cracked open like a big, broken eggshell. His combover was saturated with blood, and most of his teeth had been ejected or flushed out via the crimson sludge raining from his mouth. His malformed face was unmade by several gaping lacerations, the flaps of flesh quivering with each quake of his body.

As ghastly as the sight was, I didn't feel sick. In a strange way, I felt better. I felt the warmth—the same euphoria I had when that junk was in my veins all those years ago.

I liked it.

The final ram from the car applied enough pressure to send some of his mashed brain tissue oozing out from the cavernous void in his head like a clump of bloody sausage being squeezed out of its plastic packaging.

As I stared at the jumble of gore while it unleashed its final spasms, the warmth took over my body. The deed was done, but I started to feel strange. There was one question concerning the sick act that I couldn't seem to shake.

Am I supposed to feel this good about it?

OLD FOLKS

When I broke free of my recollection, I was still feeling the reverberations from that fateful day. I remembered that different kind of warmth in my chest as I watched him take his last breath. But as shitty as Kevin was, how did his mother feel about what happened? Did she deserve to live with the weight of her son's gruesome murder for the rest of her life? Was that fair?

I reconvened at the same conclusion that had brought me to Royce O'Riley's seminar in the first place: no.

Gotta make good, I thought, snubbing out the butt in the ashtray. *I can't live with all this on my shoulders any longer.*

I walked through the parking lot and into the building. After seeing the pictures, just being inside the place gave me the creeps. A part of me felt guilty—like if Kevin was still around, she might not be getting neglected in such a vile building. It was gaining a deep and personal understanding with those kinds of questions firsthand that had made me initially embark on my pilgrimage.

She didn't have anything to do with our issue but still suffered the consequences.

After speaking with a woman at the help desk, I was guided to a small and smelly room at the end of a hallway.

"Mrs. Fargas," the caretaker said, "you've got a visitor."

They didn't care to ask who I was or why I was there. Any semblance of policy or workplace structure was out the fucking window in Ridgeway.

The old woman sat in a fraying recliner while a small television set played reruns of *Columbo*. I could tell from watching her body shake intermittently that she wasn't in the best shape. She looked a lot like Kevin, and the way her body jerked from the spasms triggered her son's gory final moments to flash in my mind.

"Mrs. Fargas," I whispered. "How are you doing?"

She didn't say anything. She just continued to tremble and stare at the TV. I watched a cockroach scurry across the floor and climb up her chair. Before the brazen bug could mount her back, I brushed it away and stepped on it. Wiping the bug guts off the bottom of my shoe, I moved around so I could face her.

"I'm an acquaintance of your son, Kevin," I said.

"Kevin's a good boy," Mrs. Fargas whispered, eyes widening. "He comes to visit me from time to time."

I couldn't tell if she'd totally lost her marbles and was living in the past or if she was talking in a spiritual way.

"Yeah, he's—er …" I couldn't continue the lying—even the white lies. And even if it was to make her feel better. "He was Kevin … When's the last time you saw him?"

"Why, I saw him today. I'm very lucky to have a son like him." When she spoke, she sounded like she was on a cocktail of drugs. Her eyes were wide and lit up like bulbs on a Christmas tree. "He comes most days. And ever since his father died, I've been a little low on love. At first, it didn't seem right for us to show love that way, but Kevin explained how I shouldn't feel bad about it—how some sons show their mothers love like that all the time."

I peered back at her bed. It was unmade, and as I pulled the covers back slightly, I saw a condom filled with gunky semen and streaks of dried blood on the shaft. Shaking my head, I couldn't believe it.

Sick fucks.

Kevin was dead—that much I was sure of. Who could be twisted enough to slip inside this confused old woman's room, pretend to be her son, and ass-fuck her bloody?

My chest tightened with anger, making it harder to breathe.

"Everything okay in here?" a man's voice asked.

I turned to see a security guard standing outside the door. He was tall with yellow buck teeth and a pair of Coke bottle glasses. When he squinted at me, I could tell he was bothered by my presence. His security badge read: Elmer.

"Doing well, thanks," I said.

"Hey, Ma, you need anything?" Elmer asked.

"Kevin!" Mrs. Fargas shrieked in delight. "There you are! I was just talking about you. No, I don't need anything. Thank you, dear."

Elmer pushed his glasses up from the tip of his nose. "Well, chow should be coming soon."

Mrs. Fargas's wide-eyed stare returned to the television. "That's wonderful."

As the security guard made his way out the door, I grabbed him by the arm. "Why are you pretending to be her son?"

"Get your fuckin' hand off me," Elmer growled. "Not that it's any of your goddamn business, but in case you're not smart enough to put it together, she's senile. I do it out of kindness."

I nodded, holding my tongue.

"Who the fuck are you, anyway?" Elmer asked.

"I'm an acquaintance of the family," I said.

Elmer scoffed, turning away before pausing. "Some fuckin' friend you are, leaving her in this place."

As I watched him trudge down the hall, I couldn't help but feel a familiar rage. It wasn't quite what I'd felt when I lost Farrah, but it was in the ballpark. I couldn't help but think of the words of wisdom Royce had shared with me back at the conference.

Sometimes the path to atonement can only be carved out by sacrifice.

UNEXPECTED STOP

I wasn't planning on donning the black ski mask again. The last time I'd looked through those eyeholes, I'd watched someone die. But as I stared through the sliding glass door, into the house, the anger that stirred inside me was still too furious to ignore. If I was gonna make good with Mrs. Fargas, I had to deal with Elmer. But as I felt the weight of the pistol in my waistband and looked down at the gold cigar cutter in my hand, I couldn't believe what I'd decided.

I had been watching Elmer for days. While plotting things out, I'd visited the antique store again. Another unforgiving piece of steel had called to me, so I'd bought it. But this time, at the time of purchase, I knew *exactly* what it was for.

In the beginning, I was just keeping an eye on Elmer, doing what I usually did: casing his house and logging his schedule. But along the way, something changed.

As I watched Elmer reposition his daughter on the sofa, a sickening sadness intensified in my gut. His little girl seemed to have some kind of spinal condition. It wasn't just that night he'd helped her—he was *always* helping her.

Owen ... I thought, picturing my kind boy's face. *How does God let such things happen?*

Early in the morning, long before his girl's nurse arrived, Elmer cared for his daughter. And from the moment he left Ridgeway each night and for the entire weekend, he treated her like gold. And when I watched him, I could tell he cared—unfortunately I know what it's like to care for someone in such a way. He wasn't the perverted Elmer from the retirement home. When he was tending to his little girl, it was like her comfort was the only thing he cared about.

I even went out of my way to do some extra checking on him. While Elmer was at work one day, I'd called the house, impersonating a CPS agent. I spoke with the daytime nurse, explaining that Child Protective Services was doing random wellness checks on disabled children. After getting glowing reviews from the nurse, I also spoke with his daughter, Bonnie.

I curated a list of carefully worded questions. It was a test that was meant to expose that piece of shit, Elmer. Surely if he was raping Mrs. Fargas, then he was up to something horrible at home too, right?

Wrong.

The bastard passed my little test with flying colors. That little girl not only loved her daddy, but over the course of our conversation, it became clear that she deeply depended on him, and not just financially and physically. Elmer was her emotional rock. In her grim circumstances, he gave her hope.

As I peered around the oak tree, still staring through the window, so many thoughts flooded my mind. If I killed Elmer to try and make good with Mrs. Fargas for murdering Kevin, then what would become of Bonnie? What happens to a disabled girl isolated from any family with no one in her corner? The answer might've been even fouler than what became Mrs. Fargas's fate.

I'd just be starting the whole cycle again ...

It was maddening. I couldn't blame anyone but myself. I'd created a tangle of violence and pain that was just itching to ensnare more people.

No, that's not what this is supposed to be about. I visited Mrs. Fargas to make amends, not unwind another spool's worth of loose ends. Not to indirectly destroy another life.

As I waited in the darkness, I didn't know what to do. But the moment that yellow-toothed scumbag slipped outside for another smoke, suddenly, it was clear as day in my brain. When his back was to me, I crept like a black cat through the night. I was already too close by the time he felt my presence.

"What the fu—"

I swung the handle of the pistol as hard as I could. When it connected with his chest, I heard all the air in his lungs hiss out and Elmer crumpled to the ground. Squatting down at his side, I pointed the gun at his face.

"If you move one millimeter, your fucking head's gonna be all over that vinyl siding. You got it?"

Frightened and still trying to get his wind back, Elmer nodded.

"I'm here to kill you." I lifted the golden cigar cutter. "But first, I was gonna put that nasty little cock you've been sticking inside Mrs. Fargas in this hole and …" I pressed down on the device, the movement of the metal causing Elmer to wince.

"I-I'm fuckin' sorry!" Elmer cried. "I didn't realize Mrs. Fargas was connected! If I'd a known that you were a mob guy, I-I never would've touched her."

At first, I had no idea where he was getting that assumption from. Then it suddenly struck me—the end of our conversation at Ridgeway Retirement Home.

Who the fuck are you anyway? I recalled Elmer asking.

I'm an acquaintance of the family, I'd replied.

Elmer didn't sound like the brightest fella. And on top of limited intellect, I guess if you show up and try to kill a guy a few days later, drawing that hypothesis isn't illogical. I couldn't lie to him … but maybe it was best I let him believe that. Maybe it would terrify him even more than he already was.

"I'm just really lonely," Elmer continued, tears now leaking down his face. "I'm really *really* lonely, a-and I take care of my daughter all the time, so I can't find time to—"

33

I punched him in the throat and then realigned the barrel with his forehead. "Right now, I'm gonna talk, and you're gonna fuckin' listen. You understand?"

Staying with the tough guy stuff would be like throwing more gas on the fire—keeping his worst fears burning. Elmer held his Adam's apple and nodded obediently, trying to rub the pain out of his windpipe.

"But today's your lucky day," I continued. "I'm not gonna kill you ... not yet, anyway. But if you want to stay alive, three things are gonna happen." I slapped him in the face to wake him up again. "You listening?"

"Y-y-yes, sir," he managed.

"One, you go anywhere near Mrs. Fargas again, and I'm gonna take your entire body apart. Piece by piece like a fucking science project. You'll live for a while. But you're gonna wish you were dead. You're gonna beg me to stop. I will eventually, but it's not gonna be quick."

Elmer was frozen, his beady eyes bulging with fright.

"Two, you're gonna make sure no one else goes into Mrs. Fargas's room and fucks with her. And you better do a damn good job. I'm gonna be watching, ready to snatch you up at the drop of a hat."

Still wheezing from the shots I'd given him, Elmer remained obediently bobbing his head while his entire body shook uncontrollably.

"And last but not least, you're gonna take care of Bonnie. I've been watching you, and you been doing very good in that regard, but don't screw it up. If you make good on these three simple requests, your life will go on and you'll never hear from me again. But if you don't, it's gonna be a hard goodbye." As I stood and got ready to walk away, I paused my stride. "If you do the right thing for anyone, do it for Bonnie. What life would be like for that little girl without you looking after her should be enough motivation."

When I started to walk away from Elmer, I once again had to pause.

"S-s-sir," Elmer said.

I turned back. The idea of putting a bullet through his greasy forehead was still floating around up there. I still couldn't be sure if what I was doing was the right decision. Furthermore, I didn't even know if there was a right decision.

"What?"

Fresh tears ran down his cheeks. "Thank you."

Still disgusted by the man, Elmer's polite gesture only angered me more. But if there was one thing I'd learned, it was in paragraph four, chapter twenty-three of Royce O'Riley's *Live It Like You Mean It.*

Things that don't go together: lies and love, and anger and actions.

I didn't show a hint of emotion. In this situation, it was best that I kept it bottled.

"Don't thank me," I said. "Thank your daughter."

ON TO THE
NEXT

When I got home from Elmer's, I didn't feel great. The way the situation with Mrs. Fargas turned out wasn't what I'd hoped. While I do believe I helped her, it wasn't in the way I'd expected to. I imagined being able to converse and understand how my actions had impacted her on an emotional level. But she was so far gone, if I'd have flat out confessed to murdering her son, she probably wouldn't have even believed me.

Why am I complaining? I thought. *In a way, maybe it was a good thing that she believed Kevin was still alive. If that was the case, had I really even done any damage? Was it possible that she'd been off her rocker before I'd murdered her son?*

I suppose that would be the most haunting aspect. I could lie to myself and tell myself that was the case, but I don't lie anymore. The truth is that's something I'll go to my grave never knowing.

As I extracted a fresh Dart from the box and lit it up, I felt exhausted. Kevin's case was just the first in line to tackle, and I was now beginning to wonder if I had the strength to make good with all three of them.

I still can't deal with ... Addison. Not yet ... Charlie definitely has to be next. Sticking with the chronological order I initially settled on makes the most sense.

As I stared at the computer screen and took another pull, a chill ran down my spine. While Charlie's case wasn't my most egregious offense, it was no picnic. And despite taking the Kevin situation head-on, the fact that I still hadn't really confessed to anything or even heard true coherent feelings conveyed by anyone affected by the ramifications of my lies and actions scared the hell out of me.

Maybe I'll find out what it's like with Charlie.

I didn't want to think about that ordeal, but I had no choice. I'd already decided in that car outside of Ridgeway Retirement Home that part of making good was reliving it. How could I possibly be serious about it if I wasn't willing to remember every nasty detail?

Taking another drag, I prepared myself. As tired as I was, I was sure there were other people more tired than me. And I was the one responsible for their sleepless nights.

THE INTERVIEW

Farrah's funeral was a couple months ago, and I couldn't stop thinking about it. But that morning, for the kids' sake, I had to try.

The babysitter was a little late, so I was already running behind to begin with. I gave her the emergency contacts and her payment but restrained myself from giving her a piece of my mind. I didn't want a pissed-off sitter taking it out on my kids. I never imagined leaving them alone with a stranger. While I'd checked Kimberly's background out, I can never be too careful when it comes to Owen and baby Missy.

I looked at myself in the mirror one last time, making sure my tie was straight. This interview was important. As a single father of two, I was drowning. When Farrah and I were generating the family income together, we were pretty comfortable, but in the short time since she passed away, it had become clear that my job wasn't going to cut it. After many sleepless nights of filling out job applications while simultaneously trying to console grieving children, I'd finally gotten a bite.

I kissed baby Missy and told her I loved her. She answered me with a happy coo. No matter how bad my days got, those chubby cheeks always squeezed a smile out of me. I rubbed Owen's head and forced a hug on him.

"Dad, what the heck!" he cried, adjusting the video game controller and trying to keep focus.

"I love you, bud," I said.

"I love you too."

His tone was still kind of dead. I know he meant what he was saying to me, but he was dealing with a lot.

I glanced at his buddy beside him on the couch. Felix was a Hispanic kid who went to school with Owen. After many years of having a rough time making friends, I was glad that he'd found a good one. Owen needed someone outside of the family to be able to vent to. Even though money was tight, I didn't mind paying the sitter a bit extra to keep an eye on Felix too if it made things a little easier on Owen.

"Don't kick his butt too bad, Felix." I winked. "Okay?"

Felix chuckled. "You got it, Mr. O."

Instantly, I remembered I was late and didn't have time to be bullshitting.

Gotta do this for the kids, I thought.

As I made my way out of the apartment complex and into the street, my eyes started scanning for a taxi.

Should've just bit the bullet and set up a fucking Uber.

I hated the constant updates of technology and downloading new applications. The taxis had never failed me before, but now that I was late for the most pivotal interview of my life, I was suddenly having second thoughts.

As I sifted through the sea of people, I was only getting more nervous. Every time I heard or saw a car, I thought about Kevin. I still looked back fondly on the crushing hits that mashed his body against the steel pillar.

I didn't feel sad or guilty about any of it. In fact, if anything, I was a little pissed that the lemon he'd sold me was still having an impact. If the engine hadn't blown, I'd have been on my way to work instead of running around with my hand up like a desperate madman.

"Taxi!" I yelled.

When the cab screeched to a halt, I breathed a sigh of relief. I quickly slipped inside the cab and closed the door.

"Take me to Seventeenth Street, and please step on it. I'm late for an interview."

"Who's fault is that?" the cabbie asked.

I looked up from my phone to meet the man's gaze in the rearview. Below the gin blossoms on his nose and his red cheeks, he had a big grin.

"Just kidding," he said, reaching for his stainless steel coffee mug and taking a slurp.

I forced a laugh, hoping it would be the last we spoke. My eyes darted to the laminated ID card affixed to the dash that read: Charlie Martindale.

When I smelled the oversaturation of cheap cologne and heard him slurring his giggle, I quickly realized there was fuckery afoot. Of course, out of all the nasty cabs in this godforsaken city, I had to pick one with a driver that was totally tanked. Still, due to my time-crunch, I didn't have room to worry about anything but getting to my interview.

When the cab zipped off, I buckled my seatbelt out of precaution. Heart pounding, I was now nervous about more than just my interview.

Maybe since he's a little loose, he'll get me there faster. What are you saying? This is crazy. I've gotta say something ...

"Are you drinking?" I asked.

He furrowed his brow, growing agitated. "Why—" A hiccup interrupted his sentence. "W-why would you say something like that?"

"Because it smells like a bar in here and you're slurring your words."

Charlie motorboated and waved his hand as if it was the most ludicrous thing he'd ever heard someone say.

"Damn it, just be straight with me!" I pounded the seat cushion. "Can you fucking drive, or not?"

"Yeah! I can drive!"

We both fell back into a moment of silence, and he revved up the engine. But as I watched his mannerisms and noticed he was still stewing on what I'd said, I wasn't watching the road—neither of us were.

"Man, fuck you!" Charlie yelled, his eyes glaring at me in the rearview. "Who the fuck do you think you are?! This is my cab and I'll—"

Before I could scream at him to pay attention to the red light in the approaching intersection, we met with a vicious impact. And the bus smashing into the passenger side of the cab was the last thing I saw.

***

As I glared past the sidewalk full of bustling people, I could still spot him from a mile away. Charlie's swollen nose and red face glowed. After watching him for over a week, he was walking around just fine.

I wasn't really surprised—loose-bodied drunks always survived their crashes. It was probably more surprising that, aside from a concussion, I'd walked away unscathed.

Good thing I wore my fucking seatbelt, I thought.

Still, the car wreck and concussion were enough to fuck me over on my interview. I replayed my conversation with Charlie in my head.

Can you fucking drive, or not?

Yeah! I can drive!

I bit my bottom lip until I could taste a little blood in my mouth. The prick of pain helped me focus my rage. That lying cocksucker could've killed me. In a way, it wasn't much different than how Kevin had knowingly sent me out into the world with that lemon. And since I lost the job opportunity, it was almost like an attack on my children. He'd taken food out of their mouths and comfort from their clutches.

Even though we'd transitioned to the summer months, it was somehow still a little chilly out, and I still yearned for the warmth. But as much as I'd enjoyed the feeling I'd got when killing Kevin, I wasn't about to replicate it at the expense of an innocent person.

I'm not sick like those other guys who like it. I'm not an addict like my parents or like Charlie. I only do it because it has to be done.

Still, in the back of my mind, I wondered if I was stretching the definition of justice. But every time that nagging thought wormed its way back into my brain, I ignored it.

Charlie staggered away from his crumpled cab and into the convenience store. Just based on his crooked stride alone, I could see he was still heavy on the sauce.

He's been cocked every day since the accident. How can he even be fucking driving after the wreck he caused? And how is that car even street legal still?!

The answer could only be one of two things: either Charlie had blatantly disobeyed the law or he was able to manipulate the shitty system. But no matter how I sliced it, the guy was putting people at risk as long as he was on the road.

Old Charlie doesn't need his driver's license revoked ... he needs his life revoked.

As I made my way to the car, I thought about the special cocktail I'd cooked up for him. Not that I was overly worried about Charlie tasting it—his drinks were usually pretty stiff anyway—but it had crossed my mind.

In revisiting the antique store, I'd happened upon a box of vintage rat poison. That place helped me relax. It reminded me of Farrah and always seemed to have the stuff I needed—sometimes before I even knew that I needed it. Modern rodent baits are updated to ensure someone would get a nasty flavor if they accidentally ingested it, but the old recipes are pure arsenic—a tasteless killer.

Charlie's passenger side window was still broken from the accident, so it was easy pickings. The mouth of his steel mug was wide enough to dump my little mixture in without spilling it. I looked around, making sure no one was really paying attention. I unscrewed the cap, quickly reached in, and poured the vial into the cup.

As I scurried into the alley and lit a Dart, I rechecked my surroundings. They were exactly what I figured. I smiled as I inhaled smoke, knowing humanity was one big rat race—everyone was too in a rush to notice something so brief and seemingly trivial.

I'd decided to wear a hoodie and baseball cap to make my presence as discreet as possible. Keeping my head down the entire time, it had been my goal to ensure my face wasn't getting captured by any cameras in the area.

After the research I'd done, I didn't believe there to be any recording devices focused on that particular street curb, but better safe than sorry.

Charlie exited the store with a bag in his hand, just like all the other days. I was grateful to see him plop down in the driver's seat and take a big slurp of his drink immediately.

Drink up, you piece of shit.

As Charlie started to gorge on the sandwich, I thought through things again.

That fat fuck goes into the store every day for lunch and comes out with the same sandwich and newspaper. Then he sits in his car, eats, and reads for about forty minutes. That should be enough time to see it hit him.

Seven and a half cigarettes later, the show finally started. He grabbed at his chest and neck, furrowing his brow. As I watched his expression transition to shock and then panic, I could feel the warmth in my chest again.

When a little vomit started to ooze from his mouth, followed by the bubbles, it took me back. I felt like I was eight years old again, that warmth fresh in my chest for the first time as I watched Dad tremble and foam at the mouth.

That bastard. He's just like them. Mom and Dad were junkies, slowly poisoning themselves to death—Charlie's no different. I'm just speeding up the process. I had to ... I had no choice ... If I let him continue behind the wheel of that taxi, who knows how many people he'd have taken along with him.

Everything that felt so right back when I watched Dad's body shutting down felt just as right as I watched Charlie start to spasm like a manic windup doll. And in a big city filled with busy folks, no one even seemed to notice.

THE
CONFRONTATION

The house was nice—nicer than anything I'd ever been inside of. After reliving my situation with Charlie, I'd done some digging. The old lush had been married with two kids. That seemed like a good place to start.

The mother of his children might as well have been a ghost—there wasn't a trace of her anywhere. And the only thing I could find on his son, Todd Martindale, was an obituary and article about his suicide. I couldn't help but wonder if I'd played a part in his untimely decision. On the other hand, his daughter, Dorothy Martindale, had carved out quite a life for herself.

In the several days I'd tracked Dorothy, I'd watched a strong, independent woman. An organized professional with a promising career. But something was missing—no friends or love interest to be seen. As I checked the windows on the ground level, I finally came upon one that was unlocked. Adjusting my ski mask and gloves, I readied myself.

Am I really gonna do this? I wondered.

No sooner than I asked myself the question I had an answer. Paragraph nine, chapter ten.

Don't fear the outcome. The only way is forward. No matter how painful it may be, the truth shall set you free.

Royce was right. I'd come too far to go back, plus, what was I even going back to?

I slipped inside the house, and blanketed by the darkness, I made my way upstairs. When I discovered her bedroom door was unlocked, I made my way in. And before I knew it, I was quietly standing over Dorothy Martindale while she slept.

"Dorothy?" I whispered.

She remained fast asleep.

It took calling her name a few more times before she finally awoke. The confusion and fear on her face were instant.

"Oh my God, d-don't hurt me!" she squealed. "I-I have money. I can—"

"Dorothy, I'm not here to hurt you," I said gently. "Please trust me. You're not in any kind of danger, I promise."

"Then … then why are you here? A-and how do you know my name?"

"I'm here to make good. To apologize for something horrible that I did. To see what—if anything—I can do to make amends. That's all. After I say my piece, that'll be the end of it. Okay?"

She remained fearful, but I could see there was also curiosity in her eyes. "Apologize for what?"

I took a deep breath and scratched the side of my mask. I knew it would be wise to try and unpack everything in a way where I didn't immediately implicate myself.

"Some time ago, your father, Charlie … he-he did something that really fucked up my life—or at least, that's what I thought at the time."

"Welcome to the club …"

She'd said the words so quickly that the hurt in her eyes didn't even have a chance to manifest yet. I wasn't expecting that response. It threw me for a loop, causing me to pause.

"Go on," Dorothy said.

"Ah … well, without going into the details, I … I'm the one who took his life."

Dorothy didn't show any emotion when I dropped the bombshell. It was like I'd just told her I ordered a pizza.

"And you came here to confess because you feel guilty about it?" Dorothy asked.

"I must admit, my own guilt is partially responsible. But most of my motivation comes from a place of now knowing what it feels like to lose someone. How the lies that I lived were selfish and eventually ate me alive. I came here because I needed to face the ramifications and do my best to make good. But I'm a realist. I understand there's a possibility that there might not be a way for me to fix this. Even if that's the case, I'm here to find out. To do whatever I can to salvage the life that I stole from you."

When Dorothy grinned, it took me aback. What could she possibly find funny about what I'd just explained to her? But before she spoke, the grin quickly faded.

"The last thing I'd ever want to do is salvage *that* life," she whispered.

"What … what do you mean?"

"I mean that you killing my father … that was the best thing to ever happen to me."

A back-breaking burden felt like it was rising off my shoulders. I couldn't remember the last time I'd felt so light.

I shook my head in disbelief. "I don't understand."

"I wouldn't expect you to," Dorothy said. "But if you knew my father, even just in passing, then you knew he was a drunk. A *mean* drunk. A drunk who chased my mother away. A drunk who beat my brother bloody more days than not. A vile, *pathetic* drunk who forced me to live with him late into my twenties— a time when I should've been out in the world, exploring, dating, building relationships. But instead, he saw to it that I only had one relationship. I was his daughter, mother, mistress, and wife, all at the same time."

"Jesus Christ …" I mumbled. "I'm … I'm so sorry."

Tears welled up in Dorothy's eyes. She forced herself not to break down and wiped them away. "You have nothing to apologize for. You're the reason I have this life. If it wasn't for you, I'd have ended up like my brother."

Contrary to my initial assumption, it wasn't me that nudged poor Todd off the ledge. It was his old man.

Another monkey off my back.

"And while I've never been able to trust or sleep next to another man after everything he did to me," Dorothy continued, "I'm grateful I'm able to have this life. Where I have space ... Where I'm free ... Where I'm safe ... Aside from the random guys breaking into my house, that is."

We both shared a brief and very strange chuckle.

"At least you seem like a nice guy," Dorothy said.

"I'm trying."

She suddenly grew serious, almost hesitant. "This might be kind of personal, but can I ask what it was that my father did to you?"

"It feels in poor taste to speak ill of the dead. Would it be okay if I generalize?"

Dorothy nodded.

"He hurt me and my family. But that still doesn't justify what I did. *There are no ends to one's revenge.*"

Paragraph one, chapter seventeen.

"Well, I hope you and your family find peace. And I'm sorry he hurt you. Maybe if I would've done something before you did, that wouldn't have been the case."

"No, don't think like that. Regulating him wasn't your responsibility. Getting to where you are right now, that was your only responsibility. And I'm really, *really* glad that you broke free from his grasp. That you're continuing to take steps to move on what he did to you. You have no idea how much of a relief it is to know that you're okay."

She looked at me like she was about to cry again. It was like she'd needed to hear this from someone but never had.

"Believe it or not, this conversation's done even more for me. Maybe this is another turning point. Every time you come into my life ... things get better. As strange as it might sound, I've never felt as safe as I do right now."

I nodded, not knowing what to say. An awkward silence suddenly filled the room until Dorothy finally broke it.

"Before … you said that you came here to make good. I was thinking—no." She shook her head, stopping herself.

"What is it?"

"You've done so much for me already. But there is one other thing that—ah, it's too much. Forget it."

"Nothing's too much, Dorothy."

She looked down sheepishly. "It's gonna sound crazy."

"In case you haven't noticed, this entire situation is crazy. I came here to be open with you. Nothing you say is going to offend or upset me."

"Okay …"

It was like the sadness and fear in her eyes had been erased. She was displaying another emotion now—one that I couldn't believe.

"Would … would you stay the night?"

My heart started to race. She was right—it was crazy. But under any other circumstances, would it really have been?

Paragraph three, chapter two. No one can atone if they're left alone.

My heart raced, not sure if I was making a terrible mistake. But as I took a step closer to the bed, I knew there was no way I could say no to her.

THE WORST
OF THE WORST

As I pulled another Dart from the pack and lit it, I stared at the picture of me, Farrah, Owen, and Missy. My heart ached, knowing what came next. It was the worst of the worst—the last thing I wanted to think about.

Paragraph one, chapter one: several small steps equal a wide stride, I thought.

The situations with Kevin and Charlie had turned out better than I could've imagined, but I knew that couldn't be the case for my final mission. Still, I felt good about creating a much safer environment for Mrs. Fargas. And spending the night with Dorothy was cathartic for us both. I was able to give her something that she was missing. In a very strange end to the evening, I didn't take my mask or gloves off when we made love. Sure, we weren't in love—at least I wasn't— but we had love for each other, so in some ways, it was similar.

But the good spirits and elation I felt after the deed had been done, when I slipped out of her house while she slept and returned home, quickly washed away when I considered the next task at hand.

Aside from showing up and committing to this entire journey, I knew this was going to be the hardest part. But as I stared closer at our family picture and I took another drag, I knew I had to move forward.

It's unforgivable.

A sense of disgust saturated every molecule of my being as I pictured Addison's face. I decided to begin. After all, I wasn't going to be able to sleep anyway. The sooner I faced the memories, the closer I'd be to the finish line.

THE ACCIDENT

As I held baby Missy, she cried, and I cried along with her. It was like she could sense something was wrong—the same way she had when her mother had left us just a few months ago.

Owen's face was frozen, one side of it contorted into a horrible agape grimace. The continuous moan that escaped the frozen hole was followed by a constant flow of drool. Since his accident, he required around-the-clock care. He couldn't do anything for himself. I had to help him walk, help him shower, wipe his ass. Worst of all, the bright and kind boy I raised had no way of communicating.

The doctors said he could still understand me, so I usually tried to hold in my emotions around him. But with Missy going off, I just wasn't able to hold it together.

Why? I thought. *He didn't fucking deserve this!*

I blamed myself. The stress at work had gotten to me. We'd argued a few times about him getting more freedom. Being able to go out on his own and have fun with his friends on occasion didn't seem like it would be dangerous. Hell, I'd had much more freedom as kid when I was even younger than Owen. I'd made a lot of bad decisions in my day, but caving to his demands was probably the worst.

The fully dependent, speechless boy with the hideous scowl permanently stuck on his face was the end result.

My cries were interrupted by the knock on the door. I hushed Missy as gently as I could, set her down in her crib, and wiped my tears away.

"I'll be right back, bud," I said, looking at Owen.

As the knocking persisted, I closed the door to the bedroom and approached the entrance to the apartment.

"Who is it?"

"It's Felix."

I opened the door and furrowed my brow.

"Uh, hey, Felix. What are you doing here?"

"Can I please come inside? I wanted to talk to you—alone if that's okay …"

His presence had piqued my curiosity. "Okay, sure."

He stepped inside the kitchen, and I offered him a seat.

"I-I'd rather stand," he said nervously.

"What's going on? Is something wrong?"

I could see his eyes glossing over.

"I have to tell you something, Mr. O." He scratched his arm, seeming uncomfortable in his own skin. "It's about Owen's accident."

I nodded, not knowing what to say. My heart started to pump furiously, and I felt pins and needles in my fingertips.

"When Owen was in the park, when he fell off Raven's Rock and hit his head, it wasn't because he tripped—well it was, but …"

"Felix, it's okay." I did my best to reassure him and stay calm. He was seizing up. Whatever he had to say, I needed to know. "Just relax and tell me what you saw."

"There's this girl at school, she's a little older than us, Addison Woods. Out of nowhere, she started acting like she liked Owen. So she invited him to hang out at Raven's Rock. I was kind of jealous after he told me. I felt like she was taking my best friend away from me. So, I … I went there to spy on them."

I had no idea where Felix was going with the story. Each word he spoke had me on the edge of my seat.

"Anyway, it turns out that she wasn't interested in him at all. But she made it seem like she was—when they climbed up on the rock, Addison started rubbing up on him. And then ..."

I could see he was having trouble trying to get the words out, but I couldn't wait. I nudged him. "What happened?"

"And then she asked him if she could suck his dick." Tears started to well up in Felix's eyes. "He let her, but when Addison got on her knees and pulled Owen's pants around ankles, she started to laugh. And then a bunch of her friends came out of the woods, and they were laughing at him too. I think it was just supposed to be a joke, but when Owen reached to pull his pants up, he tripped. And when he fell, he hit his head really hard on the side of the rock. Then Addison pulled his pants up so people would just think he slipped."

The boy was crying hysterically, but I wasn't. I'd suddenly run out of tears.

"It wasn't right, how she lied about what happened, a-a-and what she did to Owen. So I had to tell you."

The rage inside was back, but I couldn't uncork it in front of Felix. Instead, I let the cold calmness overtake me and moved in to console the weeping boy.

"You did the right thing, Felix. You did the right thing."

"I just—I feel terrible. Owen's my best friend, a-and I feel like I should've said something sooner. But Addison said I'd regret it. She said if I said anything, that she'd make sure my life was ruined even worse than ... Owen's."

I pulled him away gently and looked him in the eye. "None of this is your fault. Whether you told someone the day it happened or if you waited until now doesn't change anything. That girl sounds scary. I'd have been scared too."

"Really?"

I nodded.

"So ... what should we do now?" Felix asked. "Should we tell the police?"

I bit my lip a moment before deciding what to say. "That wouldn't change anything. No sense in ruining two lives."

"But we can't let her get away with it, right?"

"Do you know what karma is, Felix?"

He shook his head.

"It's the belief in cause and effect. If you believe in karma, when a person does something good, it leads to more good things for them in the future. And when they do something bad, the universe finds a way of punishing them."

Felix didn't look sold on what I was telling him, and I needed him to buy it. I decided to add one more detail.

"And I wouldn't want you to get in any kind of trouble for not telling the police up front."

He hung his head and sniffled. "Okay, Mr. O."

"Do you want to see Owen for a little?"

"I don't think I can right now ... I—I've gotta get home."

His apprehension made sense to me. I wouldn't want to face my best friend either with that weight on my conscience. But as Felix turned toward the door, I grabbed his arm.

"Just one more thing before you go," I said.

"What is it?"

"Don't tell anyone else about this. Don't tell anyone that you told me. That's really important. Okay?"

I could see the confusion on his face. "Okay ... I won't."

After leading Felix to the door, I closed it. Then I picked up a chair and broke it over the dining room table.

***

As I waited in the cold darkness on the cusp of the woods, looking out at the lonely road, I felt sick. Something about this time felt different. It was somehow *more* personal than what I'd dealt with in confronting Kevin and Charlie, and yet I was still questioning what the fuck I was about to do.

Can I even actually do this? I wondered.

The gnawing uncertainty caused me to watch the girl far longer and more carefully than I'd watched Kevin or Charlie. And still, with countless clear examples of evidence that I'd seen with my own two eyes, I was still trying to dissuade myself.

That girl's a demon.

I adjusted my ski mask and balled my gloved fists, exhaling a cloud of smoke into the frigid air as my heart thudded. Calling her a demon was putting it kindly. It was astonishing to think that a lanky girl who'd just turned sixteen a few months prior—someone who'd spent so little time on this Earth—could do so much damage.

While Owen's situation was the most egregious, it wasn't the *most* egregious. During the time I was tailing Addison, there were at least another dozen boys and girls who'd fallen victim to her. These were other kids who she'd regularly interacted with who would go on to be humiliated or disgraced using various tactics. Whether it was in the flesh, like she'd done with Owen, or via calculated online campaigns, Addison was relentless in her hunger to expose those around her as inferior. And until someone taught her a lesson, no one was going to be safe.

I'd discovered that she'd started an online diary which had quite a following. Various pictures of people she'd targeted appeared, along with vicious rumors intended to tear them down. Among the many slanderous entries, I found a particularly disturbing piece.

It was about a local boy of Chinese descent named Chester Yu. Addison talked about how she'd led Chester on just to get to know more about how awful he was.

First of all, his parents are dirty immigrants who don't speak a word of English. And they're so dumb that, the few times I went to his house, I would call them different names each time. They were so stupid that they couldn't even tell. Chester went along with it, laughing with me afterward because he just wants to have sex with me.

The idiot really thinks he has a chance. I thought Chinese people were supposed to be smart. Just at math, I guess . . . Anyway, I made sure he feels like he has a chance with me so I could find out more dirt for you guys. I told him if he wanted to have sex that I'd need to see his dick first. That I wasn't going to fuck him unless it would be worth it for me.

He was really shy about it, but I got him to trust me. After he showed me, I figured out why he was blushing so much. I swear, it was basically the size of my pinky!

He definitely hasn't had sex before and don't think he's ever seen porn, because if he had, he would've never had the guts to show me his dick. Clearly he doesn't understand how weird having a dick that small is.

As I recalled the heinous note in my mind, I got angrier. It continued in even greater detail, and at the end, Addison had attached a picture of Chester from the school yearbook. And she'd also added a photo of her own tiny pinky, so there was no mistaking the pathetic nature of the poor kid's size.

The entry had over twenty thousand views.

I'd followed up on Chester. Apparently, after the popularity of the post and some additional school hazing, the boy had taken a hot bath with an X-Acto knife. After cutting his wrist down to the bone, his parents discovered him. His life was able to be saved, but he'd been on extended stay in a mental institution since the incident.

How many more should have to fall victim? It's gotta stop …

That was exactly why I was waiting in those woods. The woods that were just a stone's throw away from where that twisted girl turned my son's life into a pile of shit. Where she took him on Raven's Rock and humiliated him.

I'd watched her walk the same path every Thursday night after she left her job at the grocery store. It was a quiet stretch of road near an even quieter park. It was perfect for my plan.

I'll just scare her straight … Scare her so bad that she'll never even think of fucking with anyone again. She deserves worse … much worse. But I can't go too far. I can't keep on the path of Kevin and Charlie. Owen and Missy need me. I'm all they have left in this cold world.

But as I considered the weight of the gun in my waistband, the dark side of my mind whispered another idea to me. One that took her out of the picture completely.

No … that's too far. And even if it wasn't, it would still be too risky.

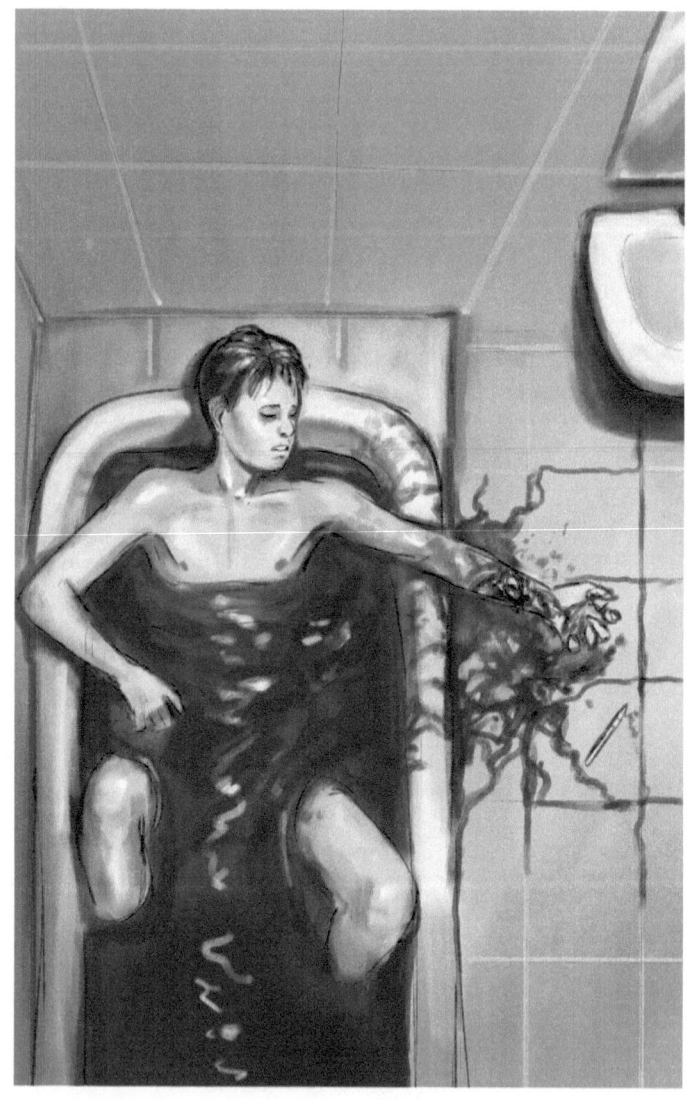

My internal battle was interrupted by the lanky teenager's stride. With her headphones on as she lazily dragged her sneakers across the pavement, I knew I needed to act. I crept from the shadows, checking to make sure there was still no one else around on the quiet street.

In what felt like a matter of seconds, I had my hand over her mouth and was dragging her into the woods. By the time I reached Raven's Rock, Addison's kicking and screaming had grown more violent. I reached for my gun and tossed her to the ground, quickly realizing something was very wrong.

Fuck, my mask!

"Get away from me!" Addison yelled.

In the heat of the tussle, she had taken my mask with her en route to the ground. When I aimed the gun at her, I soon realized that scaring her straight was no longer an option. My anonymity was no more. Furthermore, even just dragging this girl into the woods and pointing a gun at her was enough to send me away from my kids for a long time.

"Wait, you're … you're Owen's dad," she continued.

She must've recognized me from the park after Owen's accident. When the police called me, I didn't even realize she was there—everything was such a blur. Owen and Missy … what have I done to their futures?

"Don't point that gun at me!" she demanded.

I couldn't even concentrate on Addison. I instantly thought about my kids being ushered into an awful foster home. A filthy place with terrible parents—a place like the apartment I'd grown up in. If I walked away from this girl without further action, I'd all but ensured it.

"Do you know how much trouble you're gonna be in for this?" Addison asked. "I'll make sure *everyone* knows!"

It was like she wasn't even afraid of the gun. The girl was confident in her fear tactics and how she'd always been able to manipulate her way through life. She'd never faced any real consequences. Everyone who'd gotten in Addison's way had gotten destroyed, not to mention countless others who were sacrificed merely for entertainment and clout.

"If you're smart, you'll just leave now," she said. "Just fucking leave!"

I was still too shocked to speak. But another thought came to me. One that made me remember that dark path that had led me to this wicked girl. It had all happened so fast, mere weeks apart, Kevin, then Charlie, and now Addison.

I have no choice …

"I really don't think you have any idea who you're messing with …" Addison said.

I could say the same to you.

"And when you're locked away in jail, who's gonna change your retarded son's diapers?" She laughed.

The rage I was trying to bottle while I figured out the situation only bubbled inside me more violently. I could hardly control myself. It felt like I had to do something with it. It felt like it was eating me alive.

"It's too bad. Maybe your wife could've helped if you didn't let her freeze to death."

Addison's wicked eyes sparkled with clear sociopathic amusement as the words cut into my chest like an icy dagger. The cold had returned to me. It always did. But the intensifying fury inside was generating the warmth I—subconsciously or not— continued to chase. That same warmth I'd experienced on the disgusting floor of my parents' apartment as I watched my folks move on before my eyes. It was as unforgettable as the day it found me.

"When Owen told me you did that, I couldn't believe—"

Suddenly, my body had a life of its own, and it said that shooting her wasn't enough. I'd flipped the pistol around in my hand, and before I knew it, the handle had smashed into the crown of her head.

With the strike dazing her and causing blood to trickle down the side of her face, Addison slumped back. When I mounted her and wrapped my hands around her throat, it was almost like they had a mind of their own. The hollows of her eye sockets lost just a little more depth each second as I increased the amount of pressure on her windpipe.

The warmth found my chest again, urging me to tighten my grip—to wring her neck with such intensity that those glossy orbs jumped right out of her fucking head. When I listened to the inner parts of her gullet crackle and snap, I felt so damn good. Not just because I'd done a service to Owen, Chester, and the many others she'd wronged, but just because ...

***

As I held baby Missy and watched old game shows with Owen, I felt kind of good. I knew I probably shouldn't—normal people who committed such monstrous deeds would probably be sickened for life. But I suppose I'm just different.

Considering the number of people Addison had publicly hurt, I wasn't surprised that the police never made their way to me. There was no evidence of any ill will between us—as far as they were concerned, I didn't even know she was responsible for my son's accident, and neither did they.

I'd moved her body away from Raven's Rock to ensure no correlation was drawn to what happened with Owen. Under the cover of night, I'd dragged her out of the woods and left her body behind a dumpster next to an industrial building on the road she normally walked home.

Despite knowing there was no connection to be drawn between me and the crime, with her corpse just recently having been discovered, I'd gotten a terrible feeling.

It's fine, I thought. *A week's already passed. You're overthinking—*

A loud knock at the door interrupted my thoughts.

Who could that be?

I wasn't expecting anyone. I put Missy in her crib and approached the door with a raised eyebrow. "Who is it?"

"It's F-Felix, Mr. O. Would you ... um ... can you talk for a second?"

Maybe Felix was the reason I'd gotten the bad feeling. In a way, he was the only loose end. Having him show up was actually a good thing—it would give me the opportunity to check his temperature.

"Of course, buddy," I said, slowly opening the door. "You haven't been by in a—"

Seeing the long barrel of the shotgun aimed at my face stopped me dead in my tracks. I recognized the tall man standing beside Felix—tall and lanky, Thomas Woods had a similar build to his daughter.

During the weeks prior to Addison's murder, while I'd been shadowing her, I'd spied on her parents too. Both Thomas and his wife, Sharon, didn't take much interest in their daughter's affairs. Oddly enough, I knew Sharon from my childhood. We used to be neighbors when we were kids. But as I stared down the barrel of his gun, I didn't think mentioning such a trivial factoid would help me. If anything, it might make it worse.

"W-what's this about?" I stammered.

Thomas pushed Felix inside, causing him to trip and fall on the floor. Wide-eyed and bulling his way inside, Thomas nudged me back with the barrel of his gun.

My mind drifted to the kids in the bedroom.

This is bad ...

"Don't play stupid with me," Thomas growled, locking the door behind him and raising the end of the gun from my chest to my head.

"Thomas, please!" I cried. "Just relax!"

As Felix started to cry, Thomas's scowl intensified.

"If you don't know why I'm here, then why the fuck do you know my name?" Thomas asked.

Fuck!

He had me there. My nerves must've gotten to me. I used to be such a smooth liar—especially under pressure. Thomas had me on the ropes.

"But just so we're all on the same page,"—Thomas pointed the gun at Felix but looked at me—"because it's very important that you understand the motivation behind what's about happen, tell him."

Felix's crying turned into hysterics. Thomas seemed to be losing patience with him. The rage in his eyes was so familiar. I understood the intimate danger it presented.

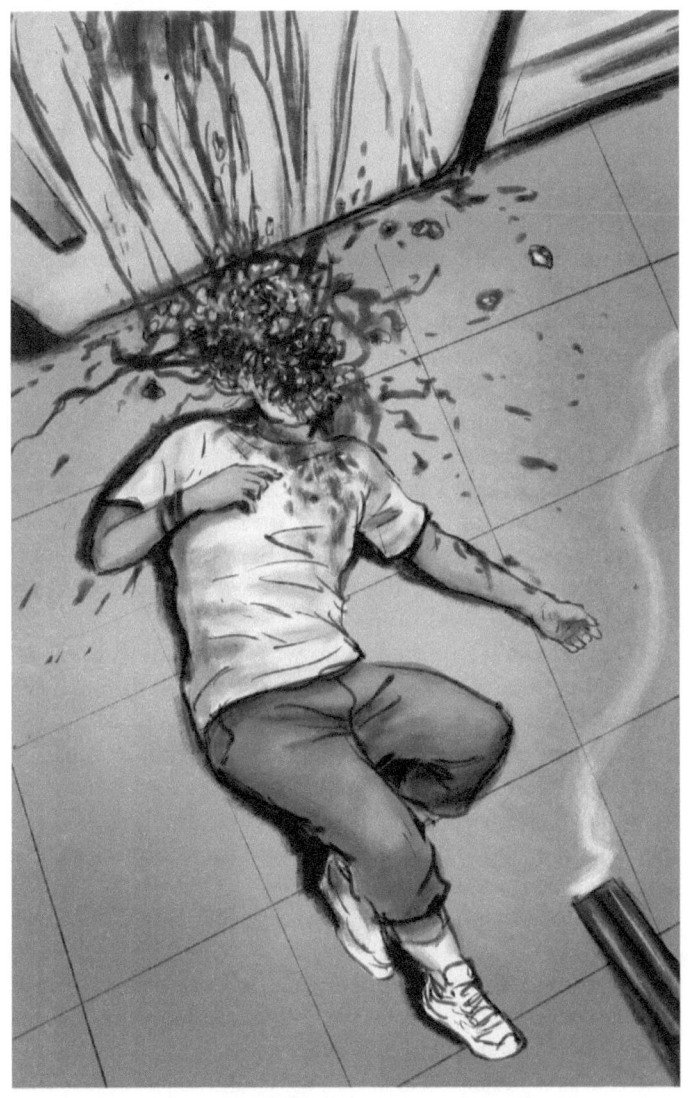

"Tell him, or so help me God!" Thomas yelled, brimming with intensity as he pumped the forestock. "Fucking tell him!"

Somehow, Felix was able to blabber the words out.

"I-I told about when I t-talked to you," Felix cried. "I s-s-said how Addison got killed just a few weeks after. I was too scared t-to tell the police, but I felt guilty. I had to tell someone. I couldn't k-keep it to myself any—"

When Thomas pulled the trigger, the barrel was close enough to Felix's face that most of the skin and meat were blown off. The splatter peppered the floor along with steel spray from the shotgun. The blast killed the boy instantly, creating a chasm of pulverized flesh in place of his frightened expression. Parts of his facial bones were exposed as a river of ruby cascaded from the void of violence that now stared back at me.

I was speechless. But it wasn't as if that mattered—clearly, this disturbed man standing in my kitchen had made his mind up. There was nothing I could say that was going to sway him. I could see that much in his eyes.

Pulling a length of rope from his back pocket, he pointed at the chair tucked into the kitchen table. "Grab that chair and let's go in the bedroom."

The last thing I wanted to do was bring him to the kids, but as he reloaded, it was clear Thomas wasn't fucking around. I had no choice.

When we entered the room, Missy was already crying. The sound of the shotgun erupting must've set her off. Owen was in his chair, emitting a distressed groan and drooling. Thomas quickly tied me up in the seat and shoved some dirty socks he'd found on the floor into my mouth.

"You're all done talking. It's my time now," Thomas whispered.

He turned and looked at Owen, who remained frozen and deeply disturbed by what was unfolding. Shaking his head, Thomas's eyes glossed over.

"It was a fuckin' accident! You could've just left it that way … It didn't have to be like this."

He was right! Why couldn't I just have left it alone!

Thomas set the shotgun on my bed and glared at Missy.

"You don't know the kind of pain you've caused ... but you will. You'll know it just the same ... maybe worse."

Reaching into his pocket, Thomas produced a clear trash bag. As he stepped toward the crib and slipped it around Missy, he glanced back at me.

"Did you know that Addison was pregnant?" He shook his head as a tear streaked down his cheek. "Just sixteen ... shouldn't have been at that age, but that's when me and Sharon had her. Who am I to bastardize my child for that? What kind of a hypocrite would that make me?"

I struggled in the chair, trying to free myself. Watching him seal the clear bag up and Missy start to cry even harder made me want to kill him. To pull each of his limbs off and smash him to a bloody pulp.

Motherfucker! Don't you dare! Don't you fucking dare!

"So ..." He twisted the end of the bag shut like a hobo would a knapsack and turned to Owen.

"I thought about this a lot," Thomas said, shaking his head. "I could've easily turned you in to the cops. On Felix's word, you'd have probably been in prison for life. But do you know the difference between that prison and the prison I've been living in every day since you took my baby?"

Several more tears rained from his face as my muffled pleas went unnoticed.

"The prison I'm inside, you never get out of. And that's what I want for you. I want you to have your freedom ... but to see what it's like when it's worthless."

Thomas whipped the bag down like he was swinging an ax. The baby smacked into Owen's face, bloodying his lips. I watched in horror as he continued with swing after swing like a madman possessed.

Each nauseating thud reverberated through my bones and rattled my soul. Each strike further turned Missy into a broken ball of blood and mangled tissue. And as Owen fell over sideways and lay on the floor, he continued to thump the gore sack into the side of his head.

As the puddle of blood expanded, I heard the groans of suffering my son expelled suddenly cease. It was then that I knew he was gone. As Thomas dumped the contents of the bag over Owen's battered cranium, a stomach-churning human sludge rained down. My sweet children, and the sole remaining legacy my beautiful Farrah had left behind, were gone. I was gone.

I instantly found myself wondering if it was my lies that had ushered this tornado of malevolence into my house. Was it those people I'd sought vengeance upon who'd really torn my family to bits … or was it me?

"Maybe I embellished the truth a little," Thomas said. He picked up the shotgun and took a seat in Owen's chair, staring daggers through me. "There is one way out of this prison. But for a selfish son-of-a-bitch like you, that's not an option. And truthfully, that makes me happy."

It was still all hitting me. The bloodbath at my feet. I could feel the comingling of Missy and Owen's blood starting to seep through my socks.

What the fuck have I done!

As I struggled to free myself, my heart felt like it was being dropped in a bowl of acid.

"It makes me happy because I want you to feel this forever. I want you to eat, breathe, and sleep it. Until you know exactly how I feel. Until you can't brush your teeth or even get out of fuckin' bed in the morning. When you realize you can't do it because it's only been about a week … but it feels like a lifetime."

He put the shotgun under his chin, carefully positioning it. More tears fell as Thomas closed his eyes.

"And I guess … that's about all I have to say …"

The shotgun erupted, turning his face into a carnal mush. Gory fragments sprayed into the air like confetti, painting the ceiling. When Thomas slumped over in the chair, a profound sense of dread hit me. But before I could even digest it, I heard a pounding on the door as the police called out.

THE HARD WAY

There is no easy way to do this, I thought. *There's only the hard way.*

As I sat outside Sharon Woods' yoga studio, I was all nerves. After her daughter and husband had visited their evils upon my children, I'd avoided contact with the woman.

When the police interviewed me, they seemed to have some odd suspicions. While I was clearly a victim, my survival certainly looked a bit strange. If or when they were able to connect me to Addison's death, there was no way to know.

I did, however, find it rather odd that when the police questioned me, they asked if I'd ever had sexual relations with Sharon. I explained that we knew each other as kids. We'd been neighbors for a few years, but that was the full extent of it. While I was grateful that a different ulterior motive for Thomas's horrendous actions had manifested, I certainly wasn't the one who'd suggested it.

Strange ... how would that idea have gotten into their heads?

The agony I'd dealt with on a daily basis truly was something special. It was the reason I'd sought out Royce in the first place. The guilt I felt for the life of lies I'd lived was suffocating me. My murderous deceptions had come back to haunt me in the most nightmarish ways.

I couldn't continue on with a black soul. I'd reverted back to the ways of my junkie parents, to that boy in high school who'd lied to everyone—only multiplied by ten thousand. Others might not have seen the blood on my hands, but I lived with it every godforsaken day.

As Sharon exited the studio and closed up, I got out of my car. There was no need for masks anymore. I was at the end of my path. There was no turning back.

This is it.

"Mrs. Woods," I said.

She turned from the door and faced me. "It's Ms. Woods now ..." Glaring at me, she unlocked the door to the studio. "Long time no see."

"Yeah."

"I was wondering when you'd come. Let's go inside."

I was highly surprised by her demeanor. Maybe she felt bad for me because her husband slaughtered my children in such a vile fashion in front of me. Maybe even more so because we'd had history as kids. But it still felt strange that she seemed to feel so comfortable with me. We weren't *that* close.

When we went inside, she brought me into her office, away from the windows.

"Forgive me, I just think it would be in poor taste for us to be seen together right now," Sharon said.

"That's fair," I agreed.

"I imagine you're here to talk about Thomas murdering your family?" she asked.

"Not exactly ..."

She was so fucking nonchalant about it. It was like she'd been desensitized to what had happened. I wasn't here to fuck around. The last pair of confrontations had left me eager to finally finish what I'd started.

Gotta make good.

"Well?" Sharon persisted.

"I have a confession to make."

She furrowed her brow.

"I killed Addison," I said.

She started to laugh. Not a minor chuckle but a deep cackle. The giggles were more disturbing than all the other reactions I'd imagined.

"The shock on your face is priceless," Sharon said. "Did you think I didn't know that?"

The confusion and pain mixing inside were propelled by my pounding heartbeat. It hadn't crossed my mind that she might be privy. I figured if she was, she'd have already informed the police.

Why keep something like that quiet?

"It seems that I'm the one with the actual confession, then," Sharon said.

My eyes opened as my heart continued to accelerate.

"While Thomas may have pulled the trigger ... I was the one who convinced him to."

The revelation felt like a hammer hitting me in the chest. Suddenly, those ravenous feelings—the primal madman ready to kill—had resurfaced.

"Immediately after you strangled our daughter—and unborn grandson—my husband was suicidal. There was no doubt in my mind that he was going to eventually kill himself. I've never been so sure of anything. So when little Felix told me about the talk the two of you had, I figured why not give him the opportunity to get even first." The hatred in her pupils burned white-hot. "For our baby ... and for her baby. An eye for an eye."

I clenched my jaw as a thousand thoughts ran through my head.

"I told the police Thomas noticed me looking at your profile on social media and suspected we'd been having an affair."

"But ... why?" I finally managed.

She pounded the desk with her fist. "Are you fucking stupid?! Because prison's not the point! If you're in a box, it won't be the same. I want you to live in that same goddamn house and hear the silence. I want you to make the same meals you did for your family but just one portion. To go into their rooms! I want you to feel *exactly* what I did!"

Paragraph five, chapter seven. The tree of choices.

Royce said to always visualize your choices like they're fruit that you're picking from a tree. To think about what you're picking clear and level-headed. That's the only way to make the healthiest choice.

On one side of the glowing tree hung a black, wilting ball of vengeance. And on the other side hung a glimmering orb of atonement. I hungered for both. If I'd wanted to, I could've walked out to the car, grabbed the pistol out of the trunk, and emptied the magazine into Sharon.

Paragraph six, chapter seven. The key to a clear mind is sleep. Instead of rash decisions, just count sheep.

Royce was right.

"Do you get it?!" Sharon continued.

"Was it worth it?" I asked.

The question seemed to take her aback. She thought about it deeply, allowing her rage to simmer down.

"No," she finally said.

"What would you have done differently?"

She again thought about it for a moment, and I could see the hurt expanding in her eyes. Her glossy orbs gazing down at a picture of Thomas that sat on her desk.

"I regret misleading the authorities." She looked back up at me. "To usher you toward the punishment you deserved, I had to tell them that I thought Thomas might've …" It hurt her to even formulate the words in her head. "That my Thomas might've had something to do with Addison's death. He was a weak man. A man who barely hung on in his normal life. But when I saw his fragile mind falling apart, it was the only way to keep you here—to force you to experience what *true* agony is."

Sharon's plan was masterfully cruel, and she was right. In a prison cell, I wouldn't have been able to have such an intimate connection to my dead family. What I'd felt during my time was a crushing weight. A weight so vicious I'd even considered taking my own life to get out from under it. But instead, I found Royce O'Riley.

Chapter nine, paragraph three. Pressure makes diamonds.

"Thomas wasn't all there," Sharon continued. "He was a lot of things ... but he would've never hurt Addison."

Her lies are swallowing her soul. If she only knew what it was like to be free.

"If I could do it differently, I'd have gone over there and put a fucking knife in your heart myself." When she spoke, there was a primal, almost animalistic quality to her growl. "Because now ... killing you is all I can seem to think about anymore."

I nodded and left the office. On my way to the exit, I could hear footsteps slowly creeping up from behind.

"Wait, where—where are you going?" Sharon asked.

Her voice sounded like, in a weird, sick way, that she'd found comfort in talking to me. And in my own strange way, I totally understood it. We were the only ones who knew the full story, and we each carried so much weight with no one to share the load. The stark disappointment was evident as I continued to head for the door.

"Don't worry," I said. "Not far."

CASHING OUT

As I looked across at the empty front desk at Ridgeway Retirement Home, I shook my head.

Where the hell she'd go? I thought. *Jamacia?*

I'd already made sure to pop in with Mrs. Fargas and check on her. The first question I'd asked was if she'd seen her son lately. She was sad to tell me she hadn't but was also somewhat happy that she could relax and watch more *Columbo* as of late.

Part of me wanted to lie about Kevin—to let her keep on thinking he was alive. But that's what started this entire mess. I was all done lying. Instead, I told Mrs. Fargas everything. She just watched *Columbo* gleefully, not acknowledging a word I'd said. But afterward, when I explained that to try and make amends, I was having her moved out of Ridgeway, to a much nicer senior living facility, she smiled. That was the only reaction I'd been able to get out of her.

I did my part. I told her the truth.

While making my way back down the hall to the front desk, I saw Elmer. There was a nervous look about him. He nodded in a show of respect. My disdain for the man had not wavered, but I was glad he'd at least been able to hold up his side of the bargain. Still, part of me wished he hadn't.

I rang the bell on the desk again. "Is anyone here?"

"What'd you want?" a woman asked, finally appearing from around the corner.

"I'm here to put in for a transfer for Mrs. Fargas," I said.

"Her POA needs to sign off on that," the woman said.

"He can't."

"Well, that's the only way."

"He's dead."

She cocked her head to the side, getting an attitude with me. "Then she needs someone else to be appointed. Otherwise, she stays here."

I shook my head, thinking about how disgusting the conditions were. While the conversation made me angry, that didn't matter.

Paragraph ten, chapter nineteen. Anger isn't a tool—it will never *help you get what you want.*

"Please, miss," I said. "All I'm trying to do is get an old lady into a safe environment. Somewhere that's clean and—"

"The rules are the rules," she said. "I could lose my job if someone found out it wasn't legit."

"She has no one to challenge it. Her family's all ... gone."

As I spoke the words, I suddenly realized that I was in the same situation. A shudder ran down my spine as I reached into my coat and pulled out an envelope.

"I have a thousand dollars in this envelope. There's a phone number on the front of it. Everything's set up already. All you have to do is call and okay the transfer."

She considered it. "I don't know. My job is worth a lot more than—"

I quickly slid the envelope toward her. "You get another two thousand once the transfer is okayed. But you've gotta do it now. Otherwise, I won't be in town to pay you the rest."

Staring at me another moment, she hesitated before finally picking up the phone. But before she dialed, the woman asked me one more question.

"You said her family's all gone ..."

I nodded. "That's right."

"Are you a friend of hers?"

Part of me wanted to just say yes. It would've been much easier to convince the woman with a lie. But I reminded myself that that version of me was dead. No matter how bad I needed it, I wasn't going to lie to get it.

"No," I said.

A confused expression overcame her as she tried to put a theory together inside her head.

"Then why do you give a damn about what happens to her?"

I felt my eyes start to gloss over. There wasn't a doubt in my mind that she saw how much it meant to me.

"Because ..." I whispered. "I'm trying to make good."

THE WARMTH

I figured I'd walk to the park. The cold's been nipping at me my entire life. What's a few more minutes matter?

I approached the mailbox across the street from the dark cluster of trees. As I extracted the bright green envelope from my pocket and dropped it into the receptacle, I couldn't help but think about the man who the letter was addressed to.

I would've never been able to do this without Royce's guidance. The least I can do is show some gratitude.

I'd spent the better part of the night penning the letter, and as it slid into the box, I felt closure. I had tied up all the loose ends—or at least I was about to. As I worked my way through the edge of the woods and into the park, I thought about Mrs. Fargas. Now, when she came to mind, she wasn't associated with a deep sensation of guilt. I thought about Dorothy. While it would've been nice to see her once more, I'm not sure it would've been appropriate.

You want that in a selfish way.

The selfless thing to do was let her keep the memory of us that we left off on. There was nothing I was going to say or do that would surpass that. Ultimately, I'd risk fucking up the good I'd done, and that would've been a mistake.

As I made my way to Raven's Rock, I thought about them all. Farrah, Owen, and Missy, of course. The family I'd built coming out of the dark shadow my parents had cast over me. Only to watch myself slowly devolve into that same bitter person. The one who lied about the horrible things he'd done to people. In the name of justice or not, the darkness and lies I lived came full circle like an ouroboros eating itself.

But now, I'd done another revolution. To the best of my ability, I tried to atone for what seemed like an impossible list of offenses. And yet, while I still felt like an utter failure, devastated by the loss of my family, I'd realized something important.

It wasn't just about me and my family.

It was about other people and learning. And it was about coming to grips with my own karma. And as I spotted Sharon standing in the darkness by Raven's Rock, I knew I was about to level mine out.

When I approached her, I slowly unbuttoned my jacket. Neither of us spoke because what was really left to say? I'd said everything I needed to on the phone while arranging our meeting. I'd given her two choices. I explained that I'd be happy to confess to the police that I'd taken her daughter's life and clear Thomas's name. But as much as she'd said how awful she felt besmirching her husband's legacy, when vengeance was dangled beside making amends, the choice was instant.

When her hand slipped inside her jacket and extracted the knife, it was smaller than I'd imagined. I felt the chill of the cold all around. The cold that I'd felt in my parents' apartment and the cold that nipped me when I'd left Farrah behind. The same cold I'd weathered the night I snapped Addison's petite neck.

But as she plunged the blade into my chest, I finally felt the warmth again. The comfort so far and few between that I'd barely tasted it. The essence of what made me human wetting my sweater as she drove me into the rock and twisted the blade. As I saw the excitement in Sharon's eyes, I was glad to be free of it. Like a sick cancer, once that darkness took hold of you, it was a long road back. And for some, there was no back.

Paragraph forty-one, chapter twenty-five. The pain is what lets us know we've evolved. Embrace it. Follow it like a roadmap. And when it's finally gone, your journey is over.

As the piercing sensation in my chest started to feel numb, the pain dissipated. Even when she pulled the knife out and stabbed me again, there was no feeling. Soon thereafter, all I could feel was the gentle caress of the warmth. And just as it had taken an epiphany to embark on my journey, I'd suddenly been struck by another. It was something I wasn't even sure was possible when I'd first started my mission, but as I felt my heart slow, I was sure of it.

No one's too bad to make good ... even me.

PART 2:
YOU'RE GETTING WARMER

BY JOHN SKIPP

YOU'RE GETTING WARMER

There is no smell like burning hair. Burnt meat, burnt plastic and paint are not the greatest. But hair holds a special place in my nasal no-fly zone: a harsh, brain-razoring wrong note in the overwhelming olfactory choir.

Close my eyes, and I still see the blaze of their faces, their crackling scalps, and howling mouths.

There's a voice like a rumble directly behind my head, on the strobe-lighting sidewalk outside Nordstrom's southeast end. I can't make out the words, but I know they're for me. I can almost feel them looking, in my synesthesia-ed brain.

Then: "Miss Mosley?" says the tall white cop, and I return him to my attention. Big man. All business. Young as me. Easily pro football-sized. I dub him Officer Linebacker.

"I'm sorry," I say. "It's just a lot." And he nods, small gesture amidst the chaos. There are more squad cars and ambuli in the mall parking lot than you'd find at your average airline disaster.

There again, I'm guessing more people just died than you

could pack in your average Boeing 747.

"Stick around," he says. "We're gonna want your statement."

"Of course," I say. "Nowhere else I'd rather be."

He throws me one-eighth of a you're-so-cute-and-funny smile out of sideways respect, and I throw it back. There ain't no substitute for a touch of gallows humor, especially when everybody else is losing their shit.

That said, it's not like he does not harbor his suspicions. How could he not? There aren't too many survivors left. And not a one of the others wearing a stars-and-stripes peace sign on the back of their fringed, vintage hippie leather vest.

I like that he's barely even trying to hide it.

If there's one thing I don't need, it's one more lying sack of shit.

***

Of course, it all started with Santa Claus. And no, I'm not talkin' about my dumbass childhood, the day I found out about poor Jolly Old Saint Nick. Although, come to think of it, it was in fact the first line of bullshit my mama ever sold me that I actually puzzled out on my own. Long after my daddy had dumped us both on account of me being mixed-race and the two of them white as cream.

But no. I'm thinking back on yesterday morning, on the TriMet bus out to Washington Square. It was an hour-anna-half from Gresham to Tigard on Portland, Oregon's public transit. Half an hour in a car. But, of course, Toby had my wheels. Again. These days, Toby almost always had my wheels.

Ninety minutes is a whole lotta time on a bus, just about every day, both ways. Fifteen hours a week of just staring out of windows, trying not to be seen. But the last ten days of riding in with Gunnar had been great, both of us traveling incognito, our respective corporate uniforms stashed in Dollar Store bags.

Fact is, I couldn't walk my ugly, hungry neighborhood streets all dressed to impress at the Nordstrom makeup counter. I wouldn't make it past the crumbling liquor store gargoyles and their sidewalk tents, much less the SWAT teams making bi-monthly raids on the drug house right off SE 206th. And Gunnar's aging, arthritic, expatriate Texan cracker ass didn't need to take any more seasonal white-bearded, weight-shaming "Ho Ho Ho!" shit off of nooooobody.

"Y'all don't wanna be wearing no Santa suit past a homeless encampment at the tail end of December," he told me the first time we spoke, once we realized we were both commuting to and from the same circles of Hell. "And God help me if somebody takes a swing or lobs a turd they just crapped in their hand. Know what I mean?"

I laughed. "Yeah, that wouldn't be good."

"I'm just sayin', the big bosses ain't hirin' me. They're just hirin' the suit. I show up with a stain, I'm back out in the rain with the rest of those miserable sons of bitches."

So it was nothing but baggy sweats, hoodies, and sneakers for us. Well, that and a seemingly endless stream of hilarious, wide-ranging, and curlicued conversations. Cuz the fact is that old peckerwood was smart and extremely well read. I didn't have a lot of friends who would talk books with me. Turns out that we didn't just frequent the same library; half the time, we were even checking out the same titles.

That's where I found out about Royce O'Riley and his Live It Like You Mean It series. These were the books that were changing my life and the reason why yesterday, I was blowing off work—a mere six days before Christmas, God help me—to attend his one-day seminar at the Portland Civic Center, with a store-bought copy of his book, *The Lies We Lay With,* sitting proudly in my lap, awaiting the great man's autograph.

Gunnar sighed and shook his head as he checked out the title, remembering this was my big day. As fate would have it, Gunnar had studied Royce O'Riley's books too. He was just a whole lot less impressed.

"So you're really gonna give this guy three hundred and ninety-nine bucks you can't afford …" he began.

"Uh-huh …"

"… to sit in a room with a bunch of suckers and listen to his bullshit for ten hours straight."

"Why, yes, I am!" I told him, grinning. "Except that I don't think it's bullshit at all. In fact, I think it's the opposite of bullshit. I think he's right on the money."

"He's right on *your* money, that's for sure."

"Oh, you're super-duper cute. Are you calling me a sucker?"

"Up until now, that thought would never've crossed my mind." We both laughed. "I mean, you're a pretty smart kid, Miss Martha Lorraine. Brains like yours don't get born every day."

"Aw, pshaw, Grampaw. That's a really sweet mixed message. So you're sayin' I'm just pretty smart for a sucker. Cuz if that's what you mean, I'd probably have to agree."

"I mean, we all make mistakes. I'm just sayin' I've seen 'em come and go. You gotta know I read my share of stupid self-help manifestos going back to the '70s, when I was your age. Mostly granola-eatin' hippie shit. But some genuine tougher stuff too."

"Sometimes, I forget you're my Grandma Daisy's age," I said. "Of course, she was super-duper cool too."

"Not like your dad."

"Fuck my dad."

"What about your granddaddy?"

"I never met him. He got killed in Vietnam. He got his draft notice just before he got to the Woodstock Music Festival, where he dropped a bunch of acid, met my grammy, and fell in love."

"Wow. No shit."

"Yeah. They called her Daisy Crockett, Queen of the Wild Frontier. She wore a coonskin cap and not a whole lot else that weekend, rumor has it."

Gunnar whistled. "I think I woulda liked your grandma."

"Well, Private Warren Mosley sure did. She says they got down in the mud and the rain and conceived my dad while Carlos Santana played 'Soul Sacrifice,' totally tripping his balls off too."

"Sounds beautiful."

"How my dad turned into such an asshole, I'll never know."

The bus stopped at a light, and Gunnar got thoughtful. Maybe he was thinking about 1969 too. Of everything he'd dreamed of and everything he'd lost. Then he looked back down at my book, shook his head again.

"I just don't see what you're hopin' to learn," he said, "that's worth all that money and sneakin' around."

"I'm not sneaking around!" I said. "Well, okay, maybe a little. I'm coming in to get my check in person cuz I don't want my boyfriend to see it. And he doesn't need to know I'm spending that much money. Even though, I mean, shit, it's my fucking money in the first place!"

"Easy, baby. You're preachin' to the drunken choir …"

"That's nice."

"Or at least the hungover."

"But I mean, seriously," I continued, on a roll. "Like, I've watched more than my share of half-baked YouTube and TikTok affirmations from the eighteen-to-thirty-year-old influencer set. The good news is that's where I sharpened my makeup skills, which leads to eighty-nine percent of my household income and easily sixty percent of my own rotten self-esteem. I mean, it is no small achievement to work your way up from a Burger King counter to a fancy-pants fashion-forward department store on the ritzy side of town, slinging four-hundred-dollar tubes of lipstick to the trophy wives of tech bros and escaped Russian oligarchs."

"It's a dirty job," he said, "but someone's gotta do it."

"Right? But it's one thing to administer relaxing facials and makeovers to the richest bitches this side of San Francisco. Quite another to be the one driving your fucking

Tesla back to the manor. You know? I got a beat-to-shit 2012 Honda Civic I hardly ever get to use because my 'boyfriend' needs to 'look for jobs' that somehow always seemed to elude him." Making the air quotes and angrily rolling my eyes.

"Sheesh," Gunnar said. "That motherfucker's still on unemployment?"

"Three months now and counting. And lemme tell ya, his measly hundred-and-eighty-six-dollars-a-week check barely keeps him in dab pens and my car in gas. Much less helping with rent and utilities."

"And how much you payin' these days?"

"Oh, it's just $1,350 a month for my wildly overpriced shithole apartment. Which he also never cleans."

"Your boy sounds like a gem."

"Don't get me started. I mean, it's not so much that I wanna be rich and pampered. I just want control of my fucking life, okay? To not be worried all the goddam time. You know? To maybe make my own hours for a change. To maybe work on things that actually matter to me. To not get bullied, or gaslit, or talked down to."

"Okay. So all you want is to be treated with respect."

"Shit, Gunnar. I'd be happy if I could just respect myself."

Gunnar nodded. "Yeah. I sure hear that."

"And seriously, thank you a whole big bunch for listening."

"Not a problem. My pleasure. And honestly? Sounds to me like you got it all figured out."

"I wish."

"I guess my point is," he said, grinning, "why the hell do you need ol' Royce O'Riley? Just write that lovely li'l three-hundred-and-ninety-nine-dollar check to me!"

"Ha ha! You wish!"

"Hell, I'll take cash, if that's easier!"

Then we both started laughing, right until I started to cry.

"Oh, no!" he said. Thought to hug me. Thought better.

"No, it's okay," I said, patting his shoulder. "You're a really good friend. I love having these talks."

"Buuuuut …" Drawing it out.

"But I gotta be honest. And with all due respect, you're not the guy I'm gonna come to for financial advice, or career management."

He chuckled, nodded. "God forbid."

"Now religious advice? Maybe. But that's the thing about Royce O'Riley. He's not like all those Prosperity Gospel jackoffs, or Manifestation morons, or all those other cosmic carpetbaggers I could fall in with if I was dumber. Royce O'Riley doesn't give a shit what I believe. Far as he's concerned, faith has nothing to do with it. Look."

And with that, I opened the book to the page I had marked. Flashed it quick at him. And then read to him out loud:

The important thing is to be honest with yourself. Simple as that. Don't lie to yourself. Don't let yourself off the hook when you catch yourself doing it.

Listen to yourself. Listen to your true self. It knows what it wants. And it knows what's real.

Once you know what's real—once you stop lying to yourself, and really listen—an amazing thing happens. You start to peel yourself free of the lies of others. Because they can be so clearly seen and heard.

Turns out the lies are everywhere, being sold to you by liars. And most people would never dare to tell you the truth, even if they knew it.

So you have to tell yourself the truth. You're the only one who can.

You're the only one who knows what's true to you …

***

"Miss Mosely," says the voice, snapping me back to the present. Not Officer Linebacker. Woman cop this time. Darker than me. Authoritative. Older. "Miss Martha Lorraine Mosely, is that right?"

"It is."

"Twenty-seven years old."

"That's correct. Yes, ma'am,"

"You work at Nordstrom?"

"Well, I did."

"You did." She gives me a look, noting the low-slung, hip-hugging bell bottoms, the vest, the little flower in my hair.

"Yes."

"But you don't now."

"Well, hell, I don't think so." I laugh. "I mean, shit." Smoke still billows through the shattered glass doors.

"Hmm," she says, not inclined to laugh herself. Unsure what to read into it. "But you were in there, right?"

"Yes, I was."

"So do you know what happened?"

"Well, I know what I saw."

She looks at me closer. "What did you see?"

"I saw," I say, "a bunch of people catch on fire."

She nods grimly. "Okay, but why? I mean how? Like, how do you think that happened?"

I shrug. "I guess you'd have to ask them."

Not even a smile. From now on, to my mind, she will go by the name Detective Killjoy.

"But, I mean, you didn't see any sources of flame."

"Nope."

"No, like, flamethrowers," adds Officer Linebacker.

"Nope."

"No bursts of flames from the air vents," he suggests more urgently.

"Nope. And nobody shooting fire beams out of their eyeballs either."

"I gotta tell you, Miss Mosley," says Detective Killjoy. "I'm really not in the mood."

"Well, I appreciate your honesty," I say.

***

So then three very fucked-up things happened, pretty much from the moment we arrived at the mall and parted ways: me toward Nordstrom, Gunnar toward the festive kiddie corral at the mall's center, seasonally known as "Santa HQ."

I didn't need to clock in, but I still needed to change into my upscale clothes before heading to the seminar. So I hit the employee dressing room, threw on my stockings and skirt, replaced my sneakers with heels, then spent half an hour with the blank canvas of my face, applying to myself the full top-of-the-line glamour usually reserved for my clientele.

It wasn't that I was trying to seduce Royce O'Riley. (Well, not exactly, anyway, much as the thought had a certain appeal.) I just wanted him to find me impressive. Or, more to the point, formidable. In the cosmetics department, and the world at large, we call it "war paint" for a reason.

And as if to make the point with the daintiness of a sledgehammer, who should waltz in but Elizabeth Lange, queen of the Luxury Men's Department. Rumor had it that she personally cleared one million dollars in sales this year, luring in the wannabe-dashing svengalis encamped at the Hilton Embassy Suites down the street as they shopped for their escorts, mistresses, or even, occasionally, wives.

Her angle was simple: "You want to look good for her, don't you? You want to…"—purring—"inflame her desires." Pretty soon, those bozos were the ones who were inflamed, falling all over themselves to impress her with the size of their shoes and wallets.

When a pair of Bruno Magli loafers runs for $400, a Boglioli Sport Coat goes for $1,455, and a simple stupid t-shirt can cost you upwards of 90 bucks, those commissions stack up fast. And God only knows how many of those Hilton Embassy Suites she'd undressed for success in herself, single-mindedly closing the sale with a black widow's elegance and grace.

Normally, Elizabeth wouldn't waste a sideways glance on me unless she needed some peon to jump and do her bidding. She was Nordstrom royalty, and she lived to be served. But as we caught each other's gaze in the mirror, I could see her little penciled-in eyebrows raise. And in that moment, miraculously, she almost saw me as a threat.

"What's the occasion?" she asked, sidling up to the station beside me.

"Oh, just another sexy millionaire. You know how they are."

"Mmm," she said. "Do I ever." Taking the opportunity to freshen up her own face. "Do I know him?"

"I don't know," I said. "Do you read self-help books?"

"HA HA HA!" she barked, grinning and shaking her head. "Do I look like I need self-help?"

"Probably not, I guess?" Shrugging. "I mean, you never know."

This was not the response she felt entitled to hear. If she had word balloons over her head, they would have read "HOW DARE YOU!"

Instead, she snapped her compact shut and sneered at my mirrored reflection. "Honey," she said, "you will never amount to shit. All the books in the world can't fix that. Ten years from now, you'll still be working that counter, if they'll still have you. But they won't, because you'll be fat."

"Huh," I said, fighting back the urge to strangle her dead as she sashayed out of the dressing room, flipping her hair like a queen's robe behind her. It figured that *"fat"* would be the worst insult she could possibly come up with.

But still, the tears came back as the door slammed shut.

Because maybe she was right. For all I knew, she was right. I was just kidding myself. My nursery rhyme name would wind up being not Humpty Dumpty but something worse—more like *Frumpty Dumptruck*—and all the Royce O'Rileys in the world couldn't put me back together when I finally fell back off of that wall again for good.

That was when my cheeks began to burn, and I could feel the heat rising up inside. It was always like that when people made me ashamed, embarrassed to even be myself. Letting their ugly voices become my inner voice. It ate away at my confidence the way Toby's voice did when he told me he wasn't fucking around behind my back. Wasn't blowing off job interviews, getting high with God knows who.

It took me another ten minutes just to repair my eyeliner damage while part of me whispered, *Why bother? Why not just clock in and cut your losses before it's too late?*

It was all I could do to stand up, look myself in the eye, and not punch the fucking mirror.

So that was the first thing.

The second one came when I finally whipped up the gumption to go down the hall and get my check, only to discover it was mysteriously a couple hundred fucking dollars short. Which was not a good thing at the best of times.

"What the HELL?" I said to Sheryl, storming into her office and practically waving the check in her face.

She flinched, as usual—as store director, she'd gradually evolved into a first-rate professional flincher—and gave me a look of such wide-eyed innocence you'd almost think she wasn't lying her ass off.

"I don't understand," she said, looking at the numbers on the check. "That should be right."

"Yeah, it should be. But it isn't. And you promised you would fix this the last time it happened."

"The last time *what* happened?"

"The last time you guys shorted me on overtime, Sheryl. Come on. Please don't make me explain it again. I don't have time. You know I have to get going ..."

"Oh, that's right. You're not working today."

"I let you know two months in advance—"

"Six days before Christmas." She clucked, trying to put me on the defensive.

"You know this is really important to me."

"I know, I know. You look very pretty."

"Thank you." Suddenly embarrassed again.

"It just makes it hard for everyone else. But no, you should go see your Ross Hoohaw or whatever—"

"Royce O'Ri—"

"Just go do your little thing. I promise I'll take care of your check. But you're coming in tomorrow, right?"

"Absolutely."

"Not missing any more days?"

"No."

"Thank goodness. And is there any chance you might be able to go a little late on Friday?"

"I …" My jaws froze in place as the impact landed.

Sheryl's eyes were still wide as a Muppet's, innocent as a Christmas babe's. But she knew. She knew what she was asking. *We're gonna stiff you on overtime, buuuuuut … could you please do more overtime, please?* With the clear understanding that, should I say no, it would go on the record against me.

I felt the warm flush as she posed the question, like my blood was welling up to poke the inside of my skin. It was the way I always felt when insult piled onto injury. Humiliated. Like I was supposed to just sit there and take it.

Was I blushing? Could she tell? I was pretty sure she could tell because suddenly, she blushed, looked embarrassed too. Told me again she'd make sure for sure I got paid. And then gave me a hug and said, "Go have a wonderful day."

It felt sincere, and then I felt bad too. Because, of course, it really wasn't her fault either.

So that was the second one. And that was bad enough.

But then it came time to cash the check, call the Uber I was splurging on, and get my ass to the seminar. Which meant parading through the main concourses of the greater Washington Square proper—a place with which I was now so familiar it felt more like home than my own neighborhood.

First thing out the doorway from Nordstrom was the little Nordstrom Annex Cafe, with Chloe and Claire sharing barista duties. They were two of the nicest, most down-to-earth people on the company payroll, simply because they had nothing to prove. No commissions. No incentive to sell sell sell. The most I ever asked of them was a blood orange spritzer with a tiny wedge of lime as an occasional treat. And it was always deee-lish.

Directly across was the T-Mobile store, featuring Fuckboy Troy with his white dress shirt and his purple dayglo tie. He was the kind of guy who probably hit on every woman in every bar he ever went to, except this bar was a mall, so underage was fair game. Now that I thought about it, he looked uncomfortably like Matt Gaetz.

Then up the straightaway, passing dozens of people I saw every day. If I didn't know their names, I knew their faces, or their hair, or their shoes, or their uniforms. Part of the bustle on display amongst the glowing storefronts, all trying to bullshit their way into our pocketbooks and hearts.

There was a new electronics store to my left, with dozens of big-screen TVs behind the massive showroom window. And on each of those screens, somebody else was lying to me. On the commercials. On the news. On the talk shows. On the game shows. In the superhero movies, where decent people were given powers and justice almost always prevailed by the end. In the music videos, where autotuning devices turned singers who couldn't sing into trilling simulations of actual emotional experience.

I took the right past the Peloton and the aptly-named Royce Chocolates, where Starbucks stared down the engagement rings of Blue Nile Jewelers and the yoga tights of Lululemon. Up ahead was the unholy red, white, and green of Santa HQ, where a line of snot-nosed rich kids already extended halfway to the parking lot.

It would be good just to see Gunnar's smiling face and wave, even if he was too busy to wave back. He was great with the kids, diplomatic with the parents or designated help. They were lucky to have him.

But when I got to the sleigh where the photos were taken—big enough to hold Santa and a family of five—the guy in the red suit going "Ho ho ho" was not my lovely Texas friend. He was scrawnier, bonier. And his face was grim behind the phony beard. No light in his eyes. No joy in his smile.

I stopped dead in my tracks, looked around to get my bearings. Were they tag-teaming Santas? How the hell would that work? *Well, honey, actually, there are TWO Santas now! You want Fred or Barney Santa? WE NEVER SAID HIS NAME WAS NICK.*

On impulse, I looked up at the food court above, checking to see if Gunnar was looking down, having stopped for a quick Philly Cheesesteak or Jamba Juice. But no. Just bored teenagers slurping their Boba teas, popping their zits, or gnawing on fries.

So I doubled around to the back of the Christmas enclosure, asked the elf-clad Mandy at the picture-printing station where the hell Gunnar was. Her eyes were sad.

"He's gone," she said. "They just gave him the boot."

"What? WHEN?" I said, vaguely aware my voice was rising.

"Like, ten minutes ago," she said. "They just gave him his check and told him to take a hike."

"But ... but why?"

Mandy sighed, her little elf-ears drooping. "Someone said he touched a kid ..."

"Oh, that's bullshit!" I said. "He would never do that!"

"I know, I know, but ..." She held up her hands in a classic *whaddaya gonna do* maneuver just as a swarm of bickering children rounded the corner, coming our way. "I'm sorry."

And that was the last of the fucked trifecta.

So I didn't even get to say goodbye to Gunnar. Didn't know if, why, or when we'd ever have the chance to ride the same bus—or any bus—again.

And it just got me so sad, put such a hurt on my soul, that I was tempted once again to blow the whole thing off. Let the force of Royce O'Riley comfort some other clown. Run down to the stop and say, *Gunnar, I'm so sorry, that's so totally unfair,* and maybe front him $100 to help him get by, even though I got shorted myself and odds were great that I would never see that money again.

But by the time I got down there, his bus would be gone. And the voice in my head had grown stubborn with rage. So instead, I just trudged past the remains of J.C. Penney, thanked God that at least I didn't work at Macy's, and headed across the parking lot to the fucking Wells Fargo.

It was time to get my cash and catch my ride.

That was twenty-four hours ago, precisely.

***

Looking back now, the seminar is a blur of heightened moments: too many to process, but each one etched like diamond on glass. A maelstrom of data both personal and totemic. A slipstream of self, deconstructed then transcended.

There is no blinking away the memory of Royce O'Riley's gaze in person. The clarity. The confidence. The piercing intellect. When you are in the room with him, there is no one else but him, no matter how many lesser men and women surround you in that space. He owns the room, from carpet to rafters. You are a bug in his amber.

And it's not his physical looks at all. On any other person, they'd be unremarkable at best. It's the intensity and focus of his energy, the raw crackling power of his presence that magnetizes all who survey him and all that he surveys.

He speaks for hours, sliding seamlessly from topic to topic, macro to micro, geopolitical to subatomic. And he doesn't just show you that all is connected; he makes you feel that all is connected. Most importantly: connected to you.

So the goal isn't to make you feel smaller than small. The goal is to make you feel like you're the center of the goddam universe. To allow the power of the universe not just to pour in but then to radiate out of you in waves.

Because it's your power, *he says to me.* Yours to channel. Yours to experience.

Yours to be.

In my mind, in this moment, I am there with him. And he is telling me that I am the only one. The true one. The one who knows. Who cannot be fooled. Who cannot be led astray.

And he forces me to confront myself. To itemize the building blocks of which I am made. To expose the rickety foundations of my disbelief, my self-doubt and self-loathing, then kick their legs out from under them, revealing the fundament beneath.

The true power of my true self.

My unbroken, indivisible self.

Then he hands me a mirror, holds it up to my eyes, has me pour myself into my own gaze. To look without blinking. Without flinching. Without fear.

Who do you see? *he asks me.* Who do you see?

And I see the tiny bundle of cells taking shape in a womb like a midnight ocean, see the DNA spiraling underneath like gossamer ribbons of infinite length, hear the ripple and clack of genetic code in motion, resonant as teletype, relaying information both forward and back through all time and all creation ...

... and I feel the mud and the rhythmic slapping, the rain and the bass and the Latin percussion, the G-spot and foreskin en route to eruption as naked Daisy and no-pants Warren fuck my poor father into existence ...

... and I know, in this moment, that my father was wrong to toss me and my poor mother out of his life. To condemn us both through character assassination, dubbing her a degenerate race-traitoring slut and me a disgusting mistake who should have never been born. He was wrong because he knew that Momma's lily-white ass did not, and never would, screw around with filthy subhuman jigaboos behind his back. Had never needed to in order to explain my existence, solve the mystery of my disgraceful mixed-race skin ...

... because I can see the sweat bead on my grandfather's forehead, and he is as black as Shaq O'Neal. But you'd never know it to look

at my cracker-ass father, who could never pass for anything but white. Who adamantly insisted his dad was white too, desperately covering for his own racist shame, the chocolate-colored gene having skipped a generation, then popped up again in the form of me ...

... and that is the first lie. The lie of my birth. The false allegation of bastardry that cast us out of the tribe before my eyes could even open. The saddle of shame strapped forever to our backs, weighing us down with its bullshit burden ...

... and from there, all the lies stack up and fall in line. All the lies that are my life, or at least the one projected on me. All the stories told of me in school. All the friends whose parents wouldn't let me sleep over and who then never quite met my gaze again. The academic opportunities I was not afforded. The clubs to which I was not welcome and would never belong ...

... and I feel the rush of power, a surge in my central nervous system, like a submarine's turbines firing up in the sprawling expanse of the Portland Civic Center. Surrounded by hundreds of others who had come in the hopes of having their lives transformed ...

I can still feel the buzz of it almost twenty-fours later: like an acid flashback, only stripped of hallucinatory defense.

The things I see now are entirely real. Could not possibly be more real.

But they couldn't have happened before today. I wasn't ready.

I'm ready now.

***

On the Uber ride home, around midnight last night, I was too fried to think straight and too wired to sleep. My mind felt comfortably numb, as the old song goes: righteously spent as a marathon runner, generating sine waves at the end of a race.

When the car pulled up out in front of my apartment, the only lights from the windows were the ones I'd set when I left. My beat-to-shit Honda Civic was nowhere to be found, though plenty of empty parking spots were available. I tipped my elderly driver handsomely, thanked her for granting me peaceful passage, sparing me the forty minutes of empty jibber-jabber I'd feared.

Then I was up the stairs, alone in my otherwise-empty apartment. Almost grateful for Toby's irresponsible absence. One less thing to explain. One less argument to wrangle.

My sleep, when it came, was dark and heavy as stage curtains. One moment I was there, and the next I was not.

But somewhere at the tail end of whatever weird dream I had, a voice I recognized as my own was calling out to me.

Remember these words, it said over and over.

The words were these:

I WILL IGNITE THE LIES INSIDE YOU.

Then my eyes snapped open to the sound of the front door softly creaking, then sliding shut.

And I knew that I should be annoyed, but I just couldn't find it in me. The whole idea that he was sneaking in just seemed so absurd, so totally childish that I had to sigh and shake my head, like watching a puppy take a shit on the floor.

I looked at the old-fangled wind-up clock—from my grandma's collection—on the bedside table. It was 6:45 in the morning. The alarm would be going off soon.

In the kitchen, Toby went to get a cup off the cabinet shelf. If he was trying to be quiet, it wasn't working out great. I chuckled at the clinking clack-a-thon, heard him furtively whispering *"Shit!"* to himself. Then I sat up in bed and said, "Glad you could make it."

"Martha?" he said. "Goddamit. I was tryin' to be quiet, not to wake you up."

"I bet. How's the three ayem job search going?"

"You'd be surprised."

"Yeah, I would."

"Oh, come on. Don't be like that."

From the kitchen, I heard him pour a cup of yesterday's coffee, pop it in the microwave, and set the timer. In the fridge, there was one splash left in the pint milk bottle, just one day past its expiration date. Not a doubt in my mind he was going to use it. Not a doubt in my mind he wouldn't think to ask first.

The alarm went off, and I let it ring for a minute, just to fuck with him. In the kitchen, he was muttering the Lord's name in vain, giving the fridge and microwave doors exaggerated slams. I counted to five, then clicked off the alarm as he made a big show of moseying slow into my bedroom, acting as if he owned the place, with a smirk of cool superiority.

"Okay," he said. "You wanna let me have it? Do your worst. Go to town."

"Honestly, Toberoo? I let you have it every day. I let you drive it around all night. Tell me, what *don't* I let you have?"

"Oh, so now you don't want me looking for work?"

"Oh, honey, " I said. "Come here a sec and look me in the eye."

"What?"

"Come here. I mean right here." I patted the edge of the bed beside me.

He paused for a second and shot me a look that would be withering as hell if I remotely gave a shit. Then he took a dramatic swig from my favorite coffee cup. WORLD'S GREATEST GRAND MAL, it read.

Normally, when Toby gave me that look, it went straight to my shame centers: immediately regretting whatever I'd done and thinking of how I might fix it. The heat would start to grow inside, my blood and stomach churning.

But now, with Royce's eyes fresh in my brain, I felt strangely cool and calm, meeting his gaze with the world's tiniest smile, almost Mona Lisa-like in its weaponized ambiguity.

"Are you coming or what?" I said, gently patting the edge of the bed once again.

"You're serious."

"Don't make me beg," I said. "Cuz I won't."

"Okay, okay. Just don't get all condescending. I fucking hate it when you get all condescending."

Yeah, that's your job, I thought, but held it back. I wanted him to sit, not flee.

Toby sat at the edge of the bed, just a few inches back from where I patted. Little gesture of defiance. Little passive-aggressive ding.

"Thank you," I said.

"Okay," he said. "So what do you want?"

"I want you to look me in the eye," I said. "And tell me what you got."

"What do you mean, 'what I got?'" Looking straight at me. Then off to the left. Then down.

"Just talk to me, Toby. I want to listen very closely."

"Why?"

"Are you afraid to look me in the eye, baby? Cuz if you are, I understand."

"What the hell is the matter with you, Martha? You think I'm afraid? Why the fuck would I be afraid?"

"You tell me," I said, smiling.

"Okay, fuck this!" he said, standing abruptly. I was starting to get to him. This was fun. "I don't know what you want me to tell you. I put in five applications this week."

"Look me in the eye and say that."

"I AM LOOKING YOU IN THE EYE!" he yelled, making a point of making ferocious eye contact. "What, are you a fucking cop all of a sudden? My parole officer? I mean, Jesus Christ!"

"You just looked away."

"I did NOT look away!" he said, looking away and then staring at me so hard he was actually gritting his teeth.

"You're looking at my forehead," I said. "Come on. Don't be a coward."

"I am NOT!" he yelled, abruptly locking eyes with me.

"That's good," I said, holding on to his gaze. "That's perfect. Now lie to me some more."

"What?"

"Or tell me who you're fucking. Either way is good for me."

He was starting to sweat, and his cheeks were flushed, and his eyes looked past me, above me, below me. "Up here," I said, pointing at my eyes, and he raked his coat sleeve quick across his forehead.

"Go to hell. Is it getting hot in here?"

"You tell me."

"Did you turn the furnace up? Cuz I don't know why, but my eyes are watering—ow!" A quick bark.

"Maybe you should tell me the truth," I said, standing since he was inching farther away. "Maybe just try it while you look me in the eye."

"I AM telling you the truth! I—OW!" And out from his mouth came a tiny puff of smoke.

"You haven't looked for a job at all, have you?"

"OW!" he repeated with a look of genuine pain. The sweat was coming hard now. I could smell it. Sweat and bourbon.

And now I could feel the tiniest crackling in the air. Like stepping too close to an electrical generator.

"Tell me you love me. And look me in the eye."

"Shut up!"

"You can't do it, can you?"

"STOP …!!!"

And then the strangest thing happened.

His whole face caught on fire.

"GAAAAAHHHH!!!" he screamed, his mouth a flapping black hole in the fireball. All at once, the smell of burning hair assailed me like a knife. I gasped and took a backwards step, trying hard to see his eyes.

Then he was running for the kitchen. And after a beat, I ran as well, following him halfway in, then steering him blindly toward the sink.

He was beating at his head with his coat sleeves now. That's when I noticed that his collar was smoking as well. I knocked a soup kettle off the stovetop, turned the cold water in the sink on full, pulled the spray nozzle end of the faucet out as far as it would go, and started spraying him in the face.

"GAAAAAAHHHHHHH!!!" he screamed again, black smoke pluming as I choked on the reek of his charcoaled goatee ...

***

"Miss Mosley!"

My eyes snap open. Officer Linebacker has one giant hand on each of my shoulders, shaking me gently, concern in his eyes.

"Oh, I'm sorry," I say. "Was I ...?"

"I think you fell asleep on your feet," says Detective Killjoy. She has no problem looking me straight in the eyes.

"Did I?"

"You were smiling."

"Hmm," I say, pretty sure that's true. The cops look at each other, then back at me.

"Are you on drugs?" From Officer Linebacker, it is barely a question.

"No," I say. And that is the truth.

"Is there something you want to tell us?" the detective asks me.

I think about that for a second.

"Are you sure you wanna know?"

They have a second to decide.

As inside, I remember.

***

This morning, I drove back to work in my own car for a change. It had been so long I almost forgot my favorite sneaky backroads route to Tigard. Missed a couple of turns a couple of times. But always worth it to avoid the seething rush hour traffic.

Only after Toby got extinguished entirely did I get a chance to think: *Whadda I wanna wear today?* If I didn't need the bus, I could dress up at home. But did I want to? Was it worth it? Did it matter, if I was really being honest with myself? And if not, what *would* matter? What was a statement worth making on this day?

By the time I made up my mind, it was time to go. But I wasn't ready. So I took my sweet time, doing my makeup just the way I wanted and sifting through my wardrobe for precisely the right thing.

The vest was an heirloom from my grandma, Daisy Crockett. The peace sign, hand-stitched. The fringes, notched with beads of bone. I'd thought about wearing it to costume parties over the years, but it just seemed disrespectful. Until today, I had never even worn it out of the house.

The hip-hugging bell bottom jeans were also hers, but I'd taken 'em out for a ride more than once. They were sassy and tight. They encased me just right. I felt both safe and savage in their embrace.

The coonskin cap was long gone, and good riddance, though I'm sure that it looked good on her. Instead, a rainbow scarf-as-headband totally did the trick. A pair of rose-colored round-framed John Lennon sunglasses perched at the tip of my nose. Feathers from my earrings. Bright love beads around my neck.

Daisy's old faded white t-shirt with the "Black Power" fist had a couple of holes under the armpits, but that just added charm. A simple suede belt and sandals, also vintage, sealed the deal.

For my eyes, I laid down just enough Egyptian Cat Lady sweep to attract attention, not cartoonishly summon the Mascara Police. Lips just red enough to show I mean it. Cheekbones just sharp enough to cut.

And then that little flower as the *piece de resistance.*

From the moment I pulled into Parking Lot 2, bottom level, one hour late, I could feel my innards tingling, guts charged and coiled as power cables. Responding to the overtures of Washington Square,

I WILL IGNITE THE LIES INSIDE YOU.

Sheryl did a double-take as I stepped onto the Nordstrom makeup floor, walking past my station, heading directly toward her. Sebastian and Nika looked up from their respective cash registers, and the expressions on their faces made their customers turn as well.

"What are you doing?" Sheryl demanded. "Don't you know what time it is?"

"Oh, you wouldn't believe what time it is," I said. "Do you have my check?"

"Your what?"

"My overtime check. You promised."

"No, I didn't—*ow!*"

"Look me in the eye and say that."

She didn't even need to open her mouth.

FOOM! Her eyes were first to burst. Her lying eyes, from the smoking holes. When she shrieked, two matching flames went up her nostrils from her lips. Then her hairspray brought the blazing sparkle to her crown.

Sebastian turned and ran. Nika stared, stumbling back. Her elderly hatchet-faced customer held a receipt in one hand and a bag full of returns in the other. I had seen that woman pull that trick before. She would not be pulling that trick again.

FOOM! The fire started at her throat, as if she'd been wearing a scarf made of gasoline and rags. It engulfed her skull so quickly it melted her dental prosthetics to her gums.

Now, customers were running and screaming, Sheryl and the old woman twirling blind, igniting racks of clothes before they tumbled to the floor. The carpet blackened at their touch.

Was I smiling? That's what the mirror said. But this whole mall was nothing but smoke and mirrors, all the way down to the rotten core.

I turned and walked toward Men's Fashion. There was someone I wanted to see.

The dressing room curtain was already ablaze when Elizabeth Lange and her stud stumbled out, a pair of torches on legs, the flesh peeling back from their burning bones. It looked as though their lies ran all the way down to the marrow. When they collapsed, they came apart like logs of ash.

And then I was out on the concourse proper, watching the whole of Washington Square burn. Screeching scarecrows in expensive clothes darted from nowhere to nowhere, banging into each other like molten bumper cars from hell. The vaulted ceilings trapped cloud banks of churning black air and particulate death, wafting wild through the halls ...

... and there was Fuckboy Troy, flaming from the balls up, whirling and shrieking with his pants on fire ...

... as I walked past the wreckage of Pottery Barn, Psycho Bunny, Victoria's Secret. Past smoldering skeleton piles, on my way down to Santa HQ ...

... and the Christmas corral was a raging inferno, the sleigh and five riders a charcoal briquette from which the sizzling remains of the fake Santa Corpse spat glistening sparks of bubbling fat ...

... and every so often, I'd see one of the living, hiding behind pillars and stone benches hotter than kilns. Their eyes sparkled with terror and something unnamable. Awe? Almost certainly. Joy? Perhaps.

These were the ones who knew truth when they saw it. Whose responses were honest whether or not their hearts were pure. These were the women who worked as janitors, mopping the shit of the scum of the earth. These were the teens selling pretzels and Jamba Juice, praying to God for a hope that was real. These were the men who'd been stripped of illusions, left with nothing but debt. Not enough to get by.

In the distance, I saw Chloe and Claire escaping out the doors together. It warmed and soothed my heart to see them mercifully unscathed.

The fire was not for them. Because they did not live on lies.

And I wanted to tell them that I did not bring the fire. That the fire was none of my choosing. That the fire was not my fault. I wanted to tell them they didn't need to be afraid. But alas, that would have been the biggest lie of all.

As I passed the immense electronics store and the rows upon rows of huge flat-screen TVs, I gazed into the overblown faces of these empty suits, sold to us as larger-than-life: the cynical pundits and treasonous preachers, neutralized news anchors and mealy mouthpieces, scheming politicians and soulless salespeople of all stripes, shapes, and sizes, all the loathsome way up to the President himself ...

... and I said to them, "Look me in the fucking eyes."

Then I watched their heads exploding from a thousand miles away.

***

Now, it's down to Linebacker, Killjoy, and me on our sidewalk oasis while the rescue teams scramble and the last lone survivors weep.

And Linebacker starts to whip out his handcuffs as Killjoy says to me, "You have the right to remain silent. You have the right to an attorney."

And I say to her, "Would you ever lie to me? Because you haven't so far, and I really respect that."

"If you do not have access to an attorney, one will be appointed by the State."

"Will it be a good one?" I ask her.

They open their mouths. The pain strikes both at once. "OW!" they say. Look at each other. Look back.

"Holy shit," she says, sweat pouring down from her forehead.

In her eyes is the question.

"You're getting warmer," I say.

PART 3:

PANTS ON FIRE

BY SHANE McKENZIE

LIVE IT LIKE YOU MEAN IT

"Who are you?"

She could hardly look at me. I kept my eyes locked onto her until her pupils finally crawled from the floor to my stare. They tried to dart away but, once I had their attention, found themselves paralyzed and at my mercy.

I watched her lips as she spoke, picking up on her hesitation.

"I … I a-am," she sputtered as her arms attempted to hide her nakedness for the third time but then fell back at her sides when she noticed the disappointment on my face. "I am Rosie … Roselyn Sanchez—"

"I did not ask for your name," I said, deaf to even my own voice but confident the words were spoken true and clearly—her expression confirmed it as I continued. "A name is only a label, chosen for you by imperfect parents polluted by their inherited dishonesty. A family tree with blackened roots, hollowed out by generations of lies like termites eating it from the inside out."

I stepped closer to her until the tips of our noses

touched, but only slightly. When she began to weep, I sighed hard enough to blow the sweat-soaked hair from her forehead before stepping away from her. Toward her husband, who stood only a few feet to her right, his body rigid and at attention like a loyal soldier preparing to receive his marching orders.

"Names can be weaponized, especially by men," I continued, feeling the apprehension radiating off the man beneath the surface, where he used his austere expression like a mask. "A test of loyalty, to publicly prove one's love and devotion. Forcing women to take their name, infecting them with the sins of their fathers, turning them into a vessel of generational trauma that will pass genetically to their children, who will grow up to repeat the same cycle, keeping the lies alive and thriving. More twisted twigs sprouting from the rotting wood of those fruitless, flowerless family trees we so desperately cling to like fungus."

As I said this, I circled the man until I was behind him. Watching as his bare skin prickled into gooseflesh, the bulging muscles beneath twitching and rippling with the anticipation of what I might do to him. But I never touched him. Stayed just a hairsbreadth above contact.

"Who are you?" I whispered into his ear before finally facing him.

His eyes locked with mine in what he perceived to be a show of strength and resiliency. Before he said a single word out loud, his mind's voice echoed through my skull. Each syllable like a hot shard of metal penetrating my brain—a pain I had grown used to over a lifetime of exposure. I didn't even wince as his thoughts invaded my head.

I need to be special. He'll see how special I am, better and more loyal than any of the others. He'll see. I'll show him.

As he began to speak, I had no need to read his lips. His thoughts were far more honest.

"I am a liar, born from a long line of liars. And I want the truth to set me free—"

114

"Lies. You want to prove your superiority. You want praise and recognition. You want the world to see you as special because deep down in your core, you know how common and insignificant you are."

"Mr. O'Riley, please, I—"

"Royce O'Riley does not exist here. It is only a label used as camouflage in a society crippled by ceremony, leaning on standard operating procedures like a crutch." I stood back so I could see both man and wife, their eyes glued to my every movement. Moths hypnotized by the light of my truth. "Here, enveloped in the magmatic truth at the very center of conscious existence, I am the Axiom."

I watched as they contemplated the meaning of their lives, no longer able to hide behind their fabrications while in the presence of such pure and concentrated truth.

"Axiom," the woman said as she stepped toward me. A bird who'd only now realized it had been trapped in a cage for all its life and who can finally see the vast blue sky just beyond the bars. "I am prideful and shallow ... a slave to vanity. I thrived off the desires of men, leveraging their lust for my own selfish gains, but even more than that, I *relished* in the jealousy of women. I used their envy like lotion to moisturize the dry and lifeless husk of my own self-worth. I needed everyone else to see me as beautiful because I could see the true ugliness underneath it all ..."

Though her words trailed off as her lips went still, I could hear her truth as if shouted through a megaphone, each word a red-hot spike being driven through my skull.

I don't want to be beautiful. I want to be true to myself, no matter how hideous it may be.

I reached out and slid my thumb across her cheek, then rubbed the waxy residue of her makeup between my fingertips. "You hide behind a colorful crust of cosmetics."

The room was dark and windowless, the only light flickering from the candles circling the feet of my potential acolytes. I turned toward the far corner where Josephine stood, waiting patiently, her mind always so peacefully silent. Using my hands, I signed to her. She nodded, already prepared as she strode toward me carrying a tray covered in various tools and utensils. She handed me a rough cloth that felt used and unwashed—an unnecessary detail. But sadism was Josephine's truth, and I was proud at how freely she displayed it. I handed the cloth to the woman.

"I want you to show me the ugly underneath."

The woman didn't hesitate as she scraped the soiled fabric across her face, wiping hard and furiously so that her skin glowed an irritated red once she'd scrubbed it bare.

"What else do you hide behind?" I asked her as Josephine stepped closer and held out the tray for the woman. I noticed a small smirk hooking Josephine's mouth as she anticipated what would happen next. Her excitement was like perfume wafting off her. "Show me who you are without the lie of beauty suffocating your truth."

The woman's expression hardened as she studied the implements on the tray. Her mind went blank, telling me she meant what she said. Her intentions were true, while her husband's were still unclear. I could feel his apprehension building as he watched his wife pick up the pliers.

When she glanced at me, I gave her the slightest of nods. As she clamped the metal jaws over the white tip of the French-manicured acrylic nail of her index finger, I couldn't help but grimace as the man's panicked thoughts erupted into a ball of fire in my brain.

I pulled my mental door shut, disengaging my antenna. A skill that took a lifetime to achieve, and one that I continue to hone and sharpen as the world's population grows more and more frenetic. A nonstop chorus of agony, the anguished screams of millions upon millions of inner demons.

With a hard yank, she ripped the acrylic nail free, peeling more than half of her natural nail off with it. Blood welled up in beads across the raw, textured flesh at the tip of her finger.

The woman stayed focused as she ripped the remaining nails off, letting them pile at her feet like bloody fish scales. Not a thought clouding her mind as she freed herself finger by finger.

I could tell by the way Josephine was scowling past me that the man was letting his feelings at what his wife was doing to herself be heard. I turned my head just slightly to glance in his direction. His lips flapped and contorted as the lie he was telling himself—that he wanted to live a life of honesty—faded away.

"Rosie, what are you—?" the man started to say, but when he noticed me looking at him, he silenced himself instantly. Got back in his military-like stance, fighting his urge to watch his wife mutilate herself.

When I turned back toward the woman, she set the bloody pliers back on the tray and picked up the scissors. With fingers spewing blood, she took hold of her perfectly layered, conditioned hair, dyed a phony platinum blond, not a single split end in sight. The dark roots were just visible, less than an inch sprouting from her scalp. And she cut it away, handful by handful, ribbons of false yellow strands raining over her feet, filling the air with its acrid smell as the hair fell across the flames of the candles. She kept cutting, nicking her skin as she trimmed as close to her head as she could, until only the natural roots were left, rivulets of blood curling around the shape of her skull and dripping from her ears and chin.

"Are you finished?" I asked her. "Has all the false beauty been trimmed away?"

She started to nod but stopped herself. Her eyes slid down her body, searching for any remnants of the liar she so desperately wanted to shed. When she reached for the scalpel with still, sure hands, I stopped her with a gentle pat on her knuckles.

"I'm proud of you. I see you," I said with a smile, then turned my head to face her husband. "I wonder if the man who tattooed his name across your identity is ready to display as much honesty as you have."

Josephine's grin widened, her teeth nearly as bright as the flames. She always took more pleasure from the agony of men—a result of her own life's traumas, but her truth all the same. She followed me with glee as I approached the man, who shifted his weight uncomfortably, still doing his best impression of a loyal dog.

"I ask you again," I said as I plucked the scalpel from the tray and held it out to him. "Who are you?"

One look at the gleaming metal edge and sweat began to bead across his flesh. A lump of anxiety bulged in his throat, and he struggled to swallow it down.

"You're right, Mr. … um, Axiom. I want to be noticed. I crave the admiration of others." His panicking eyes darted down toward his nude body, searching for something he hoped would satisfy my query. "That's why I work out seven days a week to build muscles on a body that sells insurance for a living. Muscles built for vanity rather than functionality. It's all bullshit, and I know it. And … and I want to be better."

"To be true to yourself, it is the muscles of your mind that need to be conditioned and built. Not physical strength." I forced the scalpel into his hand, his palms callused from years of gripping barbells. "There is a tendon that connects the bicep muscle to the elbow. Without this tendon, the muscle loses its ability to contract properly, robbing it of all its power."

I almost repositioned my antenna to his frequency, but the look in his eyes said everything.

"Please … Axi—Royce, don't make me do this …" He studied the blade in his hand, his eyes darting from its edge to the crook of his elbows as if trying to calculate how much pain it would cause, comparing that to the idea of failing in front of both me and his wife. His competitive nature was battling with his instinct for self-preservation.

"Cut the tendons and show me the strength of your resolve. Prove that your mind is stronger than your body."

The woman watched with a hint of disgust on her face, disappointed that her husband, the man whose name she took, was seemingly unwilling to go the lengths she had already gone. Something I had seen time and time again. When facing one's truth, it hardly ever lined up with the truths of those they once considered their life partners.

The man noticed his wife watching him, and for a moment, it was all he needed. He pressed the blade to his skin, pushed just hard enough to draw blood, but then quickly pulled away. Let the scalpel fall from his grip and clatter to the floor between his feet.

"Fuck this," he said, losing all the soldier-like body language he had been clinging to since his arrival. "And fuck you too! We come here for help, and this is what you do?!"

As he said this, he stepped out of his candle-lined circle and marched toward me. His stiff finger poked me in the chest with every word I read on his lips.

Josephine lunged at him, but I stopped her with a calm and steady hand gesture, never once taking my eyes off the man whose journey toward truth was ending before even beginning. Another liar far too addicted to deception to ever evolve. Another grain of salt in an ocean of dishonesty.

"Rosie," the man growled, speaking to his wife but keeping his eyes focused on me. "We're leaving."

When she didn't respond, his mouth curled into a snarl as his skin burned an angry maroon.

"I said we're fucking—"

Ignoring her former husband's rant, the woman picked the scalpel up from the floor before traipsing back to her circle. The flames seemed to flicker more frantically as she pressed the blade beneath her left breast and sliced it. Like a pregnant belly getting a C-section, she opened up the flesh of her mammary until it was wide enough to reach into. And then she pulled the silicone from her chest and held it like a scoop of gelatinous ice cream. It jiggled in her palm, coated in blood, more oozing from the deflated flap of skin where the breast once was.

The man gasped in horror and tried to rush to his wife's aid, but before he could get within a step of her circle, Josephine intervened with a violent thrust of her head. Her forehead slammed into the bridge of the man's nose, breaking it on impact. Blood gushed like liquid fireworks as he stumbled back and groaned.

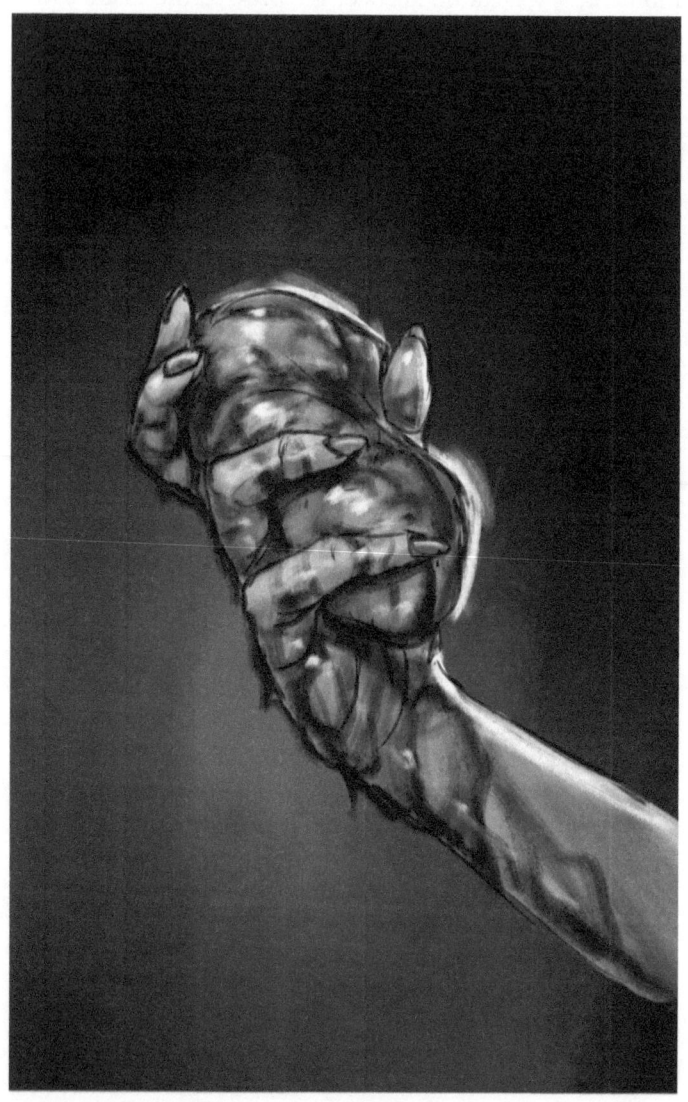

By the time he recovered and got his footing, his wife had already removed the second implant. Keeping her composure despite the pain she was surely feeling, she faced her husband and scowled with disgust.

"This is who I am," she said, then flung the implants one at a time at him, tossing them like she was trying to win a carnival prize. They hit the man in the chest, stamping him with blood before plopping and jiggling on the floor. "This is the real me. And my true self has always hated you. My true self was never happy. My true self always wished she'd never met you. Wished you didn't exist."

"And for those of us living our truths," I said, making eye contact with the woman as I signed a message to Josephine, "there is nothing stopping us from pursuing our wants and needs. Because to ignore them would be inviting more poisonous lies into our minds. And under no circumstances can we allow that to happen."

"Rosie, you can't … I love you! And you love me, goddammit! I know you—"

His eyes welled up—not tears of sadness but the tears of a child not getting the toy they wanted for Christmas. The tears of a spoiled soul not used to being rejected or being refused what they want and are convinced they are owed. Josephine had snuck behind him, the bloody scalpel in hand. And with one hard swipe of the blade, she severed both of the man's Achilles tendons, dropping him to his knees with a scream of agony.

As Josephine wrapped a strong arm around his torso from behind, holding him in place, I approached the woman with a warm smile on my face.

I gently ushered her closer to her sobbing, begging husband. Once within arm's reach, I took the scalpel from Josephine and placed it into the woman's grip. She took it willingly, and as she gripped it hard, I opened my mind to her. Zeroed in on her frequency.

I want to live my truth. I need to be who I really am. Without you.

I watched as my new acolyte drove the scalpel into the man's throat. Watched the satisfaction of enlightenment sweep over her as she pushed the blade deeper, twisting it as her oppressor's life bubbled out of him and splashed across the floor, extinguishing the candles nearest him.

Another beacon of light being birthed from the abyssal darkness of the lies that soak our world.

"Welcome to truth," I whispered into her ear before planting a light and loving kiss on her cheek.

I will never tire of witnessing these transformations. These moments of ugly truth.

THE DOMINANT TRUTH

I stood in my office, watching the television. The rest of the building had already been gutted, the furniture and books and all the rest of it moved to the island—my new commune. Where truth is God and I will be the Holy Ghost.

I tightened my left hand into a fist at my side, my other hand wiping beads of sweat from my forehead as I watched the man, my former acolyte, speaking about me on the television—words dripping with lies. Words he had been spreading around the various media outlets, gaining notoriety as the gallant whistleblower revealing the fraudulent and dastardly acts of the infamous "self-help guru" Royce O'Riley.

I wasn't afraid of the information. I tried to embrace it, telling myself that the truth, as it always did, would set me free. Yet I found my body responding to nerves as if I had anything to be nervous about.

My purpose was far too great to be floundered by the likes of this spotlight-craving heathen.

"I'm sorry," the news reporter's lips said on the screen as she repositioned herself in her chair, clearly both disgusted at what she was hearing but also ecstatic for the juicy gossip that was sure to spike their ratings. "He called them what?"

The whistleblower—his lie-given name was Richard Chapa—leaned forward, his elbows resting on his knees like a teenager telling stories at a sleepover. I watched as a satisfied smile tried to creep across his mouth, but he quickly hid it away behind his mask of insincere seriousness as his lips began forming words again.

"Axiom, which is the name he demands to be addressed as, has his *acolytes* perform bi-monthly insemination rituals. Where he watches as they—"

The television suddenly turned off, snapping to black, the only image the blurry ghost of my own reflection staring back at me with Josephine standing behind me, aiming the remote control like a pistol.

I slowly turned to face her, clenching my teeth to keep my emotional surge below the surface. A display someone as sharp as Josephine would surely assign meaning to, sparking a series of frustratingly calculated interactions in hopes of getting back on my good side.

Her hand fluttered and flexed as she signed to me, a language I intended to teach to the other acolytes once the commune was fully functional—something I had not yet told Josephine. I knew how greatly she valued our "secret language," which she assumed would be limited to just the two of us. The news would crush her, awaken the violent beast that resided within her truth. A beast that would surely feed upon the others—especially the men.

And while I took no pleasure in disappointing my loyal Josephine, I had to admit to myself that witnessing the merciless sadism she was capable of was as entertaining as any television program or fairy tale.

She would understand the importance of sharing the language. Allowing me to keep my mind closed to the thoughts of others, giving my talent a chance to rest, was paramount to my longevity. While I had strengthened my ability to disengage my inner satellite, without the proper recovery time, and as my audience continued to grow, I found myself struggling to hold the surge of voices at bay from time to time.

"Axiom," her thick, callused fingers signed. "You shouldn't worry about him. He will get what he deserves. He will be reminded how important you—"

"I don't need you to babysit me. I don't need to be protected," I signed back to her, feeling the sweat dry across my skin. "I was watching that."

"Yes … I didn't mean to …" Her hands went still, quivering just slightly at chest level before starting again. "I was only reminding you your interview begins in fifteen minutes. As you asked me to do. But if you're not feeling up for it, I can always tell him to—"

"Absolutely not," I signed with a burst of violent energy, cutting her off. I took note of the nervous step she took away from me and felt a flash of pride for my strengthening dominance over such a powerful force as Josephine. "In fact, I'm ready now. Take me to him."

"Of course, Axiom."

I followed Josephine out of my office and down the long, bare hallway. The walls were plaid-patterned with clean squares where photos once hung, all since removed. A few acolytes still worked, moving out the last boxes of my published books, each of them giving me a nod of respect as our paths crossed. Each desperate for my attention and acceptance but careful not to overstep what they perceived to be their bounds.

I blessed them with a moment of eye contact, and I could see in their expressions their gratitude for even the briefest glimpse of the concentrated truth that dwells inside of me.

As we neared the room that had been previously set up for the sole purpose of this interview, I felt my mind throb.

My talent pulsated with hunger, satiated only by consuming the private, truthful thoughts of others. A hunger that grew more and more demanding as it was deprived. A deprivation that was necessary, not only for my own sanity but to ensure I stayed in control of it. By controlling my talent, the thoughts of the outside world would not be allowed to assault me at will.

Something that had been abusing and traumatizing me since the day I was born. The very thing that led me to becoming the man—the messiah—I am today.

"Right through here, Axiom," Josephine signed as she led me toward the door.

As I crossed the threshold, I released my grip on my talent and allowed it to blossom to its full capacity.

While I would participate in this interview with full and unadulterated honesty, as I did all things, I would be in full control of it.

I let my hands fall to my sides and spoke out loud to Josephine, "Let's begin, shall we?"

LIARS' PARADISE

"Really?" Slater Davis narrowed his eyes at me and leaned back in his chair with crossed arms. "You can truly read my lips that well? You sure there's not some hidden teleprompter or something behind me?"

This asshole is full of shit. Deaf my ass ... Probably faking that deaf-tard speech impediment too. If he thinks he's gonna make a fool out of me on my own show, he's got another fucking thing coming.

"Now, Slater," I said as I matched his condescending smile and touched the tip of his knee. "This is *your* show, and I'm honored to be invited as a guest. The last thing I'd dream of doing is to deceive you."

A forced chuckle rattled from Slater's throat, his eyebrows arching dismissively. "I'd imagine so, being the self-proclaimed Prince of Veracity. Which was the title of your ... third book?"

"Fourth. And as of today, I have written nine books, with my tenth scheduled to be published just in time for Christmas, entitled *Warm Truths and Burning Lies.*"

Did I fucking ask? Just spewing more bullshit to the suckers you call fans ...

"And I'm sure it'll be every bit as fascinating as the nine that came before it. So your claim of being legally deaf, this is what you'd consider a … warm truth?"

I let a moment of tense silence fall over the room. Not long enough to be perceived as awkward to potential viewers, but just the right amount so Slater could feel it fall over him like a wool blanket.

"I have been legally deaf since the day I was born," I finally said, keeping that smile on my face as the cameraman behind Slater zoomed in on me. "During my childhood, I was called handicapped and impaired. I was told by my own mother that I would be limited in what I could achieve in my life, that I should temper my expectations of accomplishing anything meaningful … because I was different. As if my potential hinged upon verbal communication."

I did my best to hide my displeasure at the dismissive angle Slater had tilted his head.

"And so yes, Slater, I learned to read lips. I conditioned myself to speak with as few hindrances as possible so all the *normal* people around me wouldn't feel uncomfortable by the speech impediments shared by most of the deaf community. Turns out my ability to learn was just as sharp as all the other kids. Made even sharper by my need to prove my mother, and everyone, wrong."

And a razor-sharp ego to go along with it. He thinks he's better than me? I'd think with so much heat on him lately, he'd be a bit more humble. Should have been better at keeping his victims under control … like me …

I raised an eyebrow as I studied his expression. Definitely a man who had become an expert at holding a poker face.

"Did your mother ever admit that she was in fact wrong about your potential?" Slater squinted and tapped his chin with his index finger in a pitiful display of feigned interest. "I mean, with the notoriety you've accomplished and the following you've managed to create, I'm sure she's proud. What does she think of all this?"

"My mother died on my thirteenth birthday," I replied with a calm, emotionless voice. He was lying, I knew. Purposely poking at me to get a dramatic reaction for his viewers, knowing damn well that my mother had been deceased for decades.

"Oh, Royce, I apologize. I didn't mean to—"

"I made my own birthday cake that year. Strawberry with chocolate frosting." As I said this, I could taste the cake, feel the frosting coating my lips. "I sat by her bed and ate that whole cake while I watched her die. Slowly slipping away, minute by minute, staring at me with all that resentment and disappointment clouding her vision like cataracts. Never taking her eyes off me for a second as I ate forkful after forkful of moist, homemade sponge."

"Jesus, Royce, that's ... that's just awf—"

"And do you know what she told me in her final moments? To her only child? Who she swore she loved out loud while privately, in the safety of her own mind, spent every conscious moment cursing the day I was born?"

My smile widened at the silence in Slater's mind. No longer having to fake his curiosity, his thoughts were muted as he leaned forward and shook his head. It was the most honest I'd ever seen him, both in our brief interaction and on all his previous interviews I'd seen him conduct.

"She told me the truth. For the first time in her life, her physical and mental voices were united, speaking in harmony to deliver one last message. And it was those final words that changed me forever, that led me to this very room sitting across from you."

Slater wiped his palm across his face in frustration. "Well? What did she say?"

"She said that her biggest regret in life was getting pregnant with me and not aborting me while she had the chance."

"Good lord, was she truly that harsh? And on your birthday—?"

"That's the thing about truth, Slater. It can be harsh and abrasive and covered with sharp thorns. But to deny that would be to deprive yourself of the perfumed, velvety beauty that can blossom from it."

I saw a flash of doubt flicker over Slater's face while at the same time noticing an equally potent flash of inspiration sweep over the cameraman's expression, pulling his eye away from the camera as the epiphany spread through him.

"She told me that raising me, a deaf and timid child who was bullied mercilessly and crippled with social anxiety and post-traumatic stress, had robbed her of true happiness. She told me that no matter what anyone else thinks or what society says I'm supposed to do or care about, to be honest with what I wanted and who I really was. Even if others would look down on it or judge me for it. In the end, living a life of lies only leads to regret and pain."

"Is that right?" Slater's expression contorted back to his usual mask of superiority. "And is that what you've done with your life? Found true happiness?"

At the expense of others.

I leaned forward again, making him lean away from me. Watching his expression as I touched his knee, a bit harder this time. "You want to ask me about the allegations."

"And what makes you say that, Royce?"

Without the allegations, you wouldn't be worth my time, you fucking philandering phony.

"Because not only can I read lips, but I'm pretty skilled at reading facial expressions and body language as well." I slapped his knee this time, chuckling as I did it to make it seem friendly, but I could tell by his reaction that he felt the frustration behind it. "And because I know what your viewers really want. They want to be titillated. They find no entertainment value in truths and honesty or putting in the work it takes to truly discover one's happiness. They thrive off the gossip and deceptions peddled by the media, broadcasted directly into their living rooms to enjoy with buttered popcorn."

"Well, Royce, I don't know if that's accurate … or fair."

When I didn't respond, Slater shifted his weight, crossing and uncrossing his legs. The silence torturing him.

Fighting against his instinct to fill a void with noise, no matter the sincerity of its source.

"But I guess when you're right, you're right," he said, leaning over and slapping my knee even harder than I'd slapped his—a petty little revenge he seemed to take some satisfaction from. "The allegations against you by Richard Chapa are pretty severe. And yes, our viewers want to hear your perspective. Are they true?"

"That is a question not so easily answered, Slater. Real honest-to-God truth cannot be defined, as it is unique to each and every individual." I said this knowing it would frustrate him. Knowing it would incite his more aggressive journalistic nature.

"So you don't deny it? Is that what you're telling me?"

I knew it was true. A true professional would have never let any of that come to light. He would have stayed in control ... the way I controlled Amy and all the others ...

"Deny what, exactly, Slater?"

"That you're a fraud. You talk about truths, but it's all a ruse to manipulate your audience and get rich off their traumas and desperations. Using them to get at their families, pulling them into your orbit so you can gain full control. Even children ..."

"There is nothing fraudulent about living my own personal truth. I only intend to guide others to do the same for themselves. Including their families or anyone else who I think has potential to evolve. My truth cannot be theirs as yours cannot be mine." Another knee touch, but I held my hand there. I could see how badly he wanted to swat it away. "I will not, however, refute the claim that I intend to financially benefit for my goods and services. You and I are no different when it comes to that, wouldn't you agree, Slater?"

You dare compare me with you?

"And how is that, exactly?" he asked as he subtly shifted his knee away from my touch.

"You yourself have a new book that's only recently hit the bestseller list, is that right?" I watched him squirm and couldn't help but smile. "A list I've inhabited myself ... nine times. A list that comes with certain economic benefits."

"I ... that wasn't the reason I—"

"You owe no explanation or apology for being rewarded for your work. If you can supply something that people desire, then you are providing a service. That's what we are, you and I, after all. Service providers. I suspected this interview was a marketing ploy to help sales. To keep your name on that coveted list. Am I right?"

You motherfucker ... You think you can control my interview? You think you can try and make me look stupid on my own fucking show?

"I apologize if I've hijacked your show, Slater." Another knee touch, but this time, I gave him a pat like a good little puppy. "You go ahead with your questions. I imagine you've got plenty more."

"There's been rumor of some kind of secret island. How true is this?"

"I don't know if I'd call this a secret, Slater. This is a commune, a place for my community to be together. A place where we can grow and help one another in a safe and nonjudgmental environment."

Slater nodded and grinned, seemingly satisfied as if I'd just given him and his viewers exactly what he'd hoped for. He leaned forward again, his elbows on his knees. His grin widened and his eyebrows arched.

"As I'm sure you heard, Richard Chapa accused you of some pretty horrendous things. Do you have anything to say about that?" Though it didn't seem possible, his smile widened even more. "Particularly what he said about what he called insemination rituals."

I only smiled back and matched his body language. Locked eyes with him, which made him uncomfortable and lean a bit away from me.

"Now, Slater," I said through my toothy grin. "As a fellow public figure, you should know better than to ask me something like that."

"Because it's false, or because you don't want to answer the question?"

"My community is made up of those who live their truths, Slater. And as far as I'm concerned, that's what really matters."

Knee touch. I smiled as I watched his jaw muscles bulge with agitation.

"Speaking of truth," I said, my eyes piercing his, "who's Amy?"

THE PRINCE OF VERACITY

"For those of you who seek the truth," I said as I faced the crowd and lifted my arms to them, "I want to see you. Stand up, show yourself. Today, if you so choose, can be the last day you let the falsehoods of our society control who you are or how you present yourself."

There was a moment of still silence, as there always is when I present this idea to a collection of individuals. All still stuck in their habits of conforming to the many. Blending in with the mob.

As usual, there are those who eagerly stand immediately, shooting judgmental glances at those who remain seated. These attention-seekers are never as honest as they'd like others to assume they are. These, like so many, are lying to themselves about how true they desire to be.

But I smiled at them, giving them a dose of that special attention they so desperately seek. I listened to them, a hurricane of thoughts washing over me. Voices layered upon voices, assaulting my brain like a swarm of angry wasps. Yet I can pick out the truly special ones.

This is why I'm here ... what am I so scared of?
Stop being such a coward and let yourself be seen!
For Christ's sake, what is wrong with me?

I allowed a full minute to pass in silence, observing my potential acolytes. Mentally cherry-picking the individuals I saw as valuable additions to the commune.

And as they always do, person by person, those who possessed the true intention of finding who they really were, who wanted to step out of the darkness and into my light, began to find their courage and stand.

"Don't be afraid of who you are. Of who you want to be," I said as I made eye contact with the few truth-seekers. Even the ones who still lacked the confidence to stand. I saw them—I heard them. "There is nothing wrong with you. That apprehensive feeling stirring in your guts in this moment is your addiction to lies. Weighing you down so heavily that you cannot even stand from your chair. Release yourself. The weightlessness of truth can set you free, allow you to float above all the deception that floods our world. And I promise you, once you are above it, you can see it more clearly. Not only the lies but the truth."

He's right. I don't want to be this person anymore. I want to be better.

This is what I need ... to change. To be anyone but the person I've become.

My smile widened as more stood from their seats and faced me. One at a time, I made eye contact with them. And those who locked stares with me, I knew they were special. I knew they would be valuable assets for my plans, for all the work that had to be done.

Hundreds of others stayed seated, clutching their books, just waiting for me to stop talking so they could rush the stage and watch me scrawl my false name across the title page. So they could brag and display my signature on their bookshelves, never intending to read the text with any true intention of soaking in the information.

"I see you as you see me," I said to them, giving each of my future acolytes a few seconds of individual attention. Locking onto them as their frantic and panicked thoughts went silent. "Today is the first day of your true life. Only once you've accepted and embraced your true self can you truly begin to live. And I am honored to be your shepherd."

As I stepped off the stage, the largest yet on that specific tour, I watched as many of the liars who had so eagerly hopped to their feet started to doubt their own honesty. Their knees wobbled beneath the weight of their lies as I passed by them, not blessing them with even a moment of my attention.

While this seminar had been the largest so far, it was the final stop on my tour that I anticipated the most. A stadium with over two thousand seats, every one of them sold. I knew, of course, that most of those seats would be filled with liars parading as truth-seekers, but for the dozens among them who truly wanted truth, they would be the final addition to my commune. To my personal island filled with acolytes, not only worshipping my truth but basking in their own purity. Discovering who they really are and, as a result, evolving into loyal soldiers who would be invaluable in the incoming and ongoing war against a society fueled by deception, led by those who fed off the despair and desperation of the very people they fed their lies to like slop in a pig's trough.

As I walked among them, ignoring the constant noise of the unimportant who clogged the audience all around me, I zeroed in on the silence.

"How about you?" I asked a woman with thick eyeglasses and a wig that sat slightly off center on top of her head. "Do you seek the truth?"

To my delight, she remained silent both mentally and physically as she nodded. Her magnified eyes averted to the floor, but I reached out and lifted her face by the chin until our gazes met again.

"I know you do," I said to her through a grin. I held it there a moment until her mouth stretched into a genuine smile, one dripping with need. Not a need to fit in or to please me but a need to find the truth. "I see you."

"I have read all your books," she said, her lips moving so slightly that I had to focus on every twitch of her mouth in order to read the words they timidly formed. "I know you are the one who can show me the way. I know you'll lead me to the truth where so many others have lied and betrayed me."

In that moment, her mind opened up and revealed her darkness. I didn't hold it against her. I knew the effect of my presence, how it tends to tug on repressed memories, pulling them kicking and screaming into the light.

Like my father ... Night after night ...

His special princess needed special attention. No matter how many times I begged him to stop. No matter how hard I cried ... or bled ...

I moved my hand from her quivering chin to her palm. I felt her flinch a bit, but she ultimately accepted it. While touch was something I tended to avoid, I knew it was the key to this woman's truth. And nothing is more important or valuable than that.

As I led her from her seat toward the stage, she didn't resist. I knew she was truly special when we climbed the stage and faced the crowd and her mind went silent again. Not because it was hiding her demons but because it was ready to accept change, embrace the light.

She reminded me of Josephine, a poor lost soul that had been wounded by a lifetime of lies, traumatized by the dishonesty of the people around her, those she assumed loved and cherished her but whose true intentions were to feed on her.

When she looked up at me expectantly, her wig shifted a few more inches, but she did nothing to correct it. Those massive eyes blinking, waiting for me to make all the pain and suffering disappear.

"I am going to ask you a question, one I'm sure you've asked yourself countless times in your life. A question that, up until this very moment, you may have been too scared to answer."

I let another tense silence hang in the air, a silence so powerful that all those who stood initially found themselves lowering to their chairs. And all who remained on their feet were those who would soon be joining my community.

"Who are you?"

***

"Daddy's princess …"

"And why is that?" I asked as my foot ground her wide glasses to sparkling dust beneath my weight—we were alone in a bare room backstage. "Why did Daddy call you his princess?"

She struggled to speak through her blubbering lips, her face glistening with tears, saliva, and snot. It all mixed together and dripped off in stretchy ribbons.

Without her glasses, her eyes were crossed, the left one twitching uncontrollably like a broken wind-up toy. I knew without those glasses, she couldn't see me. I was just a blurry shape in front of her. A flurry of swimming colors in the shape of a man.

In the shape of Daddy.

"H-he—I w-was special, he said."

"And were you?"

She paused, starting to close off. When her mind started to scream and beg, I tuned out. Focused on her pitiful face. It made me so sick that I reached out and snatched the wig off her head and held it out to her like a fresh scalp.

She reached for it, crying harder now that her bald, scabrous dome was exposed. Covered in wounds where she'd clearly been picking at herself as if trying to dig the bad memories from her skull.

"I'm—I'm not special. I-I'm garbage. Always been garbage … And he—"

"He made you feel special."

"No! I wanted him to stop! I begged him, but—"

"You lie," I said as I ripped strands of hair from her wig and tossed them at her, making it stick to her wet face as she blubbered harder and harder. "You wanted to feel special. You wanted to be a princess."

"No, I—"

"You wanted your daddy to come to your room. Wanted to be the damsel awaiting her savior. And so you did and said exactly what you needed to, right? So you could be Daddy's special princess and stop feeling like garbage."

She dropped to her knees and sobbed at my feet, clinging to them, spreading her snot and tears across them as she bawled.

I bent down and forced the tattered wig back on her head. I admit she brought out the animal in me.

I don't like being wrong. I was sure this woman had true potential. But she was right—she was just garbage.

I forced her to look at me again with her crossed eyes, knowing she couldn't see me. Knowing that at that moment, I might as well have been her father.

"Now," I said, "show me what he did to make you feel special."

THE LIES WE LAY WITH

As the plane soared over the city, I watched as the buildings, the cars, and all the people shrunk into dollhouse sizes. All the wandering citizens marching in lines without realizing it, each and every one of them an ant serving their queen, which was their own blissful ignorance.

The stewardess tapped me on the shoulder, her smiling face reflecting back at me from the glass of the plastic window. I turned and returned her smile and read on her lips that she was offering me something to drink.

"Grape juice would be wonderful," I told her with a light touch to her elbow. I could feel her wanting to pull away, her mind telling me that the men she served on these private jets were always reaching for her, always prodding at her body without her consent. And the types of men who could afford to fly on a jet such as that were always important types, big wigs and fat cats who could potentially ruin her career if she were to displease them. Or even her life, the lives of her loved ones, if she were to voice her displeasure at their touch.

And so rather than pulling away, she allowed my fingertips to make contact with her bare elbow. I could feel the velvety moisturizer spread across the rough skin, could smell its flowery scent.

"Sorry if I made you uncomfortable," I said as I pulled away from her and smiled wider. Her mind told me how much she appreciated that. "I can't imagine what you must endure in a job like this. Are you happy?"

She blushed, trying her best to hold on to that smile she was surely trained to keep plastered across her face at all times, no matter the circumstance, in the presence of customers and clients. But as she stared into the truth behind my pupils, as my eyes injected peace and the comfort to even allow her to speak freely, that smile melted away like margarine on warm bread.

"I used to be," she said through a nervous chuckle. "I love to travel, love to meet people. For a while, this job made me happy. But I don't know … It was never supposed to be so … permanent. I'm thirty-three now and—"

"What would make you happy?"

She started to tell me. When her lips went still, her mind erupted into thunderous chatter that I struggled to keep up with. This was a restless mind, one so riddled with regret and inner demonic possession that it was like a chorus of voices all screaming out at once, each one of them with a different opinion about what it was that would make this woman truly happy.

I turned off my antenna. Not because I couldn't handle her but because it needed its rest in order to strengthen its barricades once we arrived at the island. With the commune now so full of acolytes and potential members desperate for my affection and acceptance, it would be a mental assault far more intense than any seminar or workshop.

If I want to keep my mind closed to the battering rams of their thoughts, I need to let my talent recover properly.

The stewardess's professional grin returned, stretching the tension off her expression, flattening out the wrinkles of worry webbed across her skin.

"Now you stop that, Mr. O'Riley," she said, and this time, she touched me. Playfully slapped my arm, touching me just long enough to imply a flirtatious motivation. "I know who you are, you know. Always getting folks to open up their hearts and spill their guts to you. But me? I've got other things to worry about than bothering you with my problems. Like a nice glass of grape juice."

Part of me wanted to force her to sit across from me so we could discover her truth together. Not because she was special but because of the way she seemed to be dismissing me, as if the truths I could expose her to were of no interest to her.

As if she had better things to do than crawl free from the prison of the falsities weighing down her pursuit of happiness.

"If serving me juice will bring you as much satisfaction as it will for me drinking it, then I wouldn't dream of standing in your way," I said, reaching out and touching her elbow and holding my touch there long enough to watch her squirm before finally pulling away. "And if you could please put that in a glass filled with ice. As full as you can get it."

"Yes, Mr. O'Riley, sir. Anything you like."

I glanced across at Josephine, who was sipping a bottled water, room temperature, to be sure. She clutched a bright green envelope with my name written sloppily across it— another fan letter, no doubt. She had clearly been watching my interaction with the stewardess, surely picking apart every word and gesture. A loyal second hand, to be sure, but incessantly petty and greedy with my attention.

"You sure you want to drink grape juice before we arrive at the commune?" she signed to me. "You know grape juice gives you heartburn. Maybe a ginger ale or a club soda—"

"Your grape juice, Mr. O'Riley." The stewardess handed me my drink wrapped in a warm cloth napkin. I wasn't sure if she'd used the napkin to soak up the condensation or to block our skin from making contact again.

I took the glass with another smile and sipped it immediately. The acidic taste washed over my tongue and bathed my pallet in virgin wine.

"Thank you very much ..." I trailed off, asking for her name without asking for it.

"Vivian," she said through her teeth, the corners of her mouth twitching as she fought to hold that damn smile.

"Thank you, Vivian. I think the two of us will be just fine for the rest of the flight," I said, then took another long, satisfying drink, letting the juice sit and moisten my upper lip like a kid with a Kool-Aid smile. "Why don't you go ahead and put your feet up? You've earned a break, don't you think? We all need to rest sometimes."

I watched as she tried to interpret my words, expecting some prophetic message to be hidden. I like to do that sometimes, just to shut the demons up. A little confusion and curiosity can go a long way.

As I sipped my grape juice, I made sure to give Josephine a good hard look over my glass. When I licked the purple mustache from my lip, she finally turned away. Tossed her nearly-finished water to the seat beside her as she peered out her window.

"Any word on our good friend Slater Davis?" I asked to the back of her head, though I could see her watching me through the reflection on the window.

"His book is being pulled from shelves as we speak, nationwide," Josephine said, looking at me over her shoulder so I could read her lips. "And his name has officially fallen off the bestsellers list."

I laughed and sipped my juice. "Good work."

We sat in silence for a few minutes before she turned excitedly toward me again.

"Axiom," she said, all hurt feelings aside. Her expression now with a hint of enthusiasm. "We've arrived."

I emptied my glass and crossed the aisle so I could sit next to Josephine. My own excitement carried me toward and beside her. She beamed at my presence, like a daughter whose father was finally showing interest in her.

"Isn't it beautiful?" she asked, her sigh fogging up the glass enough that she had to wipe the condensation away.

As I watched the small island come into view, its shape like the skull of some undiscovered tropical creature, my heart swelled inside my ribcage. The trees swayed in the breeze, the water so blue it was like a rippling mirror reflecting the sky back at itself.

"It is absolutely breathtaking." I gestured toward the postcard. "What is that?"

She held it up as if to hand it to me but then set it beside her on the seat instead, not wanting to share my attention with whoever it was who'd written the letter. "Something I thought might inspire you, another person whose life has been so positively affected by your wisdom. But for now, let's just concentrate on this moment ... okay?"

When Josephine's hand slipped itself into mine, I thought about pulling away. Skin-to-skin contact generally repulsed me, something I only allowed when absolutely necessary. But for some reason, in that moment, it felt right. It felt necessary. And when I gripped her hand harder, the smile she flashed at me was one I hadn't seen since the day I ushered her into her truth.

We stayed that way as the plane began to lower, circling the island as it descended bit by bit. The closer we got to the island, the more detail I was able to make out. The green foliage, thick and thriving in this special place, hidden away from the rest of the world.

A pure, honest place. A place where the concept of deception was washed away by the tides, blown away by the winds of truth. I saw the sparkle and shimmer of schools of tiny fish flowing with the force of the currents. Herds of miniscule little souls being pushed and pulled without realizing it, following the actions of the majority because to stray away from the norm would leave one alone and exposed to the hungry, toothed cruelties of those who dwelled in the darkness of the outside. Those who followed the rumbling of their truths to fill their bellies and bloody their fangs.

It was only when the plane landed and our sweet and lovely Vivian opened the door latch did I see the herd of people awaiting our arrival. Each one with a toothy smile that was equal parts excitement for my presence to step onto the sand of our new home and their own desperation to please me. Little did they know, a man such as myself would far prefer—and respect—an honest sneer over a forced smile.

Each of them wore the scars or small disfigurements that were a direct result of their evolution from liar to honest. Every one of them unique, proving to me they were ready for enlightenment, worthy of joining me on the island.

But as I studied their faces, I couldn't help but think back to that woman at the seminar. How wrong I had been about her potential.

How wrong I had been about Richard fucking Chapa ...

Since the beginning, I made it a point not to remember any names of my acolytes because I know that names are the first lies given to us—I don't allow my own name to be muttered there.

A man with a crooked, dark scar across his cleft lip, one he once hid behind a thick bushel of facial hair, stepped up before the crowd. His smile was so wide that his lip parted to reveal his gums as he approached me with his hand out.

From his body language, it was obvious he felt comfortable with me, which was evidence that we'd had multiple interactions in the past. While I recognized his face—specifically his honest imperfection—I struggled to find any memorable moments in my mind between me and this man.

If you know me so well, you'd know better than to extend that moist hand to me.

"Axiom," Cleft said as his nervous eyes bounced from his hand to my expressionless face. He finally read my energy and pulled his hand away. Glanced embarrassingly toward the others behind him before making eye contact with me again. "Welcome to the island."

"We are all so pleased that you're finally here to see all the work we've put in to making this place exactly to your specifications," a short, squat woman said, scars ground into her flesh where I'd made her remove her various tattoos with coarse sandpaper. "To start the tour, we'd like to show you the—"

"The Axiom needs to rest," Josephine said, stepping between me and the others like a security guard blocking a horde of fans trying to mob a pop star. "Please show us to his quarters."

Cleft and Scar exchanged a quick look, their eyes dripping with disappointment. They each shot a glance toward all the others waiting shoulder to shoulder behind them before finally turning and facing me and Josephine again. Then their expressions stretched back into their false, people-pleasing smiles.

"Of course," Scar said before turning to the others and making a gesture with both hands, causing the crowd to part and make a path, their backs to the palm trees.

Cleft then positioned himself between me and Josephine and the rest of the people present there at the landing strip. "Please, Axiom," he said before his upper lip twitched like a rodent sniffing out a meal. "Follow us."

THE POWER OF HONESTY COMPELS YOU

As Josephine worked on me, I shut my eyes and aimed my face toward the ceiling. I had many moments in my life when I was grateful for being deaf. The most important by far was the ability to mute the falsehoods that spilled from the mouths of the countless sheep that made up the ever-growing flock of society.

Another, though, was the wet, sloppy sound of Josephine's palm stroking the shaft of my cock. While I had never had to endure such a sound, I could tell by the violent motion and gelatinous substance she used to lubricate her palm that our monthly milking ritual was anything but silent.

Not only for my own sake but for Josephine's as well, I made sure not to make eye contact or even glance down at her while she worked. This, as we'd both agreed, was a necessary evil. A task neither of us took any joy from—which was why Josephine was perfect for it.

My seed, as crude as I found the whole process, was important. Not just to the commune and my acolytes but to the world at large. For every wriggling sperm was packed full of concentrated truth with the potential to make great change in a world desperately needing evolution.

To deny the world the chance to evolve was cruel and went against my own personal truth. My honest desire to help and usher society away from the lies and toward the brightness of truth was my one and only purpose on this Earth. And I am willing to go the lengths required to fulfill that purpose, no matter how unpleasant it may be.

Josephine, who had a dark past with men, had enthusiastically agreed to assist me in this, though I could see in her eyes that she was repulsed by the very idea of it. But she was following her truth, which held a desire nearly as strong as my own to spread the word throughout the land. To save the many souls caught in the web of deception like so many helpless flies awaiting their venomous death.

As I felt myself growing closer and closer to climax, my mind began to wander. I tried to stay focused on the positives, tried to find peace and happiness with the idea of the island, filled with acolytes working hard to bring my vision of a new world to life. A dream of mine for so many years finally becoming a reality, to set foot on my own piece of land, the truest earth to ever rest my weight upon.

I tried to focus on all the new souls we'd be saving, all the truth-seekers I'd managed to touch throughout my most recent tour, a tour the likes of which I'd never imagined when I was first aware of my great purpose. A tour that was filled with sold-out venues and eager people fighting for the right to sit before me and soak in my knowledge.

Yet my thoughts wandered, zeroing in on the whistleblower—Richard Chapa. As my orgasm rode my pleasure receptors and worked its way from the base of my testicles and up the shaft where Josephine worked, focused on her task, it was Richard Chapa's smug smile that flashed through my mind.

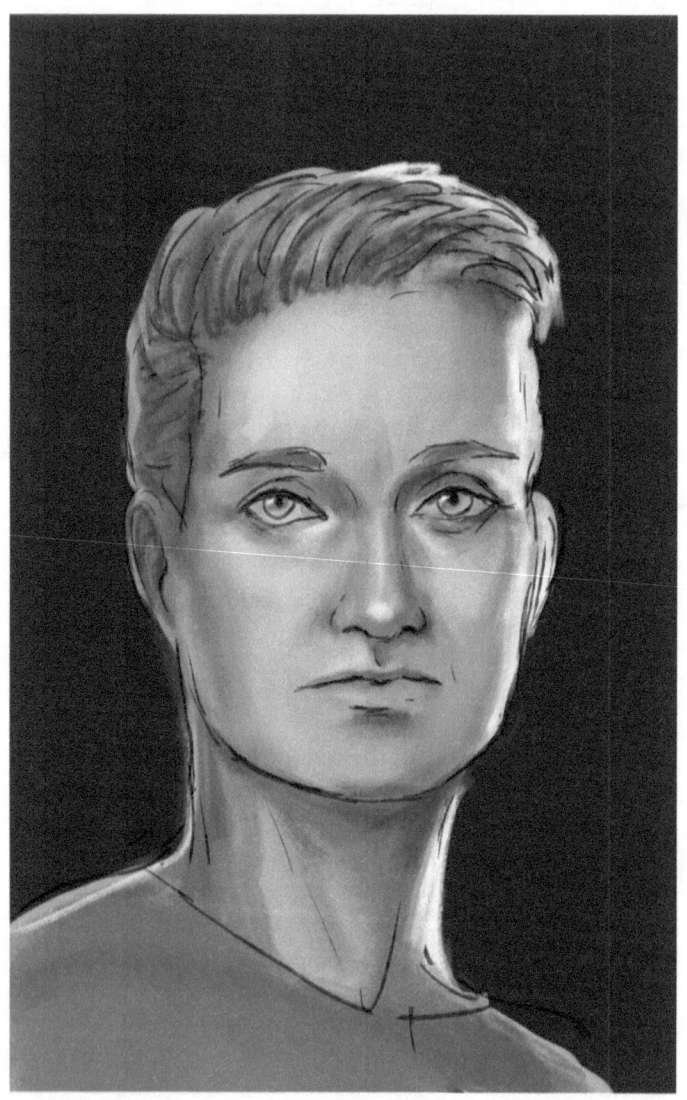

I ground my teeth and clenched my fists. Knowing that this man was going around and trying to undo my truth with his lies boiled my blood. I knew I couldn't stand for it, knew I had to do something drastic to make an example out of him. Not because I had a specific grudge against this man—he was doing what most of society was taught to do. He was using lies as weapons to benefit his own existence, taking the lessons I had personally taught him and contorting them into unrecognizable shapes and displaying them to the masses in hopes of realizing a level of success that not only matches my own but neutralizes it.

I had to make an example out of this man to prove to my acolytes that such lies, especially those using pure truth as their base, cannot and will not be tolerated.

They needed to see that I, their Axiom, their Holy Ghost, was the one and true light that would lead them through the violent darkness that shadowed their existence. And that all other lights were false and dangerous, could lead them into the jaws of predators or off the edge of a cliff to plummet deeper into the dark than ever before.

And as this thought swept through my tense and anxious mind, I felt the orgasmic surge reach its height.

During our milking rituals, Josephine and I had an arrangement. She would do what was necessary and I would endure it so we could produce the seed that would help lead our community into the future. To make sure that seed was properly handled but, also of equal import, avoid any unnecessary unpleasantries.

In my moment of heated inner turmoil, I had forgotten to warn her of the incoming surge. I had forgotten to give her time to not only gather the specimen receptacle but make sure she was safely out of range.

By the time I had realized my mistake, my seed was already splashing across her face, hanging from her nose and lips in pearly ribbons. And my loyal Josephine didn't so much as bat an eye.

Embarrassment and shame swept across my flesh, turning my skin warm and red as I stared down at her in horror, watching as she wiped off the seed with her hands and transferred the ruined, compromised life essence across the fibers of a towel.

I signed to her, "I apologize, Josephine. I was lost in thought and got carried away."

"There is nothing to apologize for," she signed back, her fingers glistening with white strings stretching between them. "Let's get you cleaned up and we can try again."

As she signed this to me, I could see her fighting the urge to display her revulsion. Even through this, she managed to keep her mind clear and true.

"You are truly a loyal companion," I said to her out loud as she used the towel to wipe off the last pearl of cum that bulged from the tip of my cock. "I am lucky to have you."

We waited thirty minutes in silence, standing side by side, before she began again.

FIBBERS INC.

"The children begin their day with a nutritious breakfast each morning before their daily enrichments. Music, art, physical education," Cleft said as he led me through the cafeteria, weaving between tables filled with children of all ages. "They get a thirty-minute lunch between lessons. Today is spaghetti and meatballs. Are you hungry, Axiom? The food is excellent, if I do say so myself."

The children did their best not to stare as I made my way through them. Clearly instructed by the adults, probably taken through drills to make sure they got it just right.

I made eye contact with a young boy, between ten and twelve years old. Unlike the others, he didn't look away. The girl with pigtails beside him even drove a sharp elbow into his side, but he didn't waver. I sat beside him, the little girl gasping and quickly scooting to make room for me.

"What do you think?" I asked him. The sound of my voice must have snapped him out of whatever trance he'd fallen into because he suddenly looked away from me, his hazel eyes locked onto the red pasta in front of him. "Is the food as excellent as he says?"

The boy glanced at me once, quickly, before snapping

back to the spaghetti. He shook his head, a few of the others around him either snickering or nodding in agreement.

"No?"

"I mean …" he started, "I guess it's not horrible, but it's definitely not excellent."

"It's horrible," another child said from across the table, inducing a chorus of whispers and gasps I could see on the lips of the children all around me.

Cleft and Scar shared a look of frustration before starting toward the tables as if to assign punishments. Before I had to make a move, Josephine darted toward them, signaling for them to back off. Sometimes, I wondered if I wasn't the only one who could read minds.

They quickly fell back, keeping their eyes on the floor as Josephine placed herself between them and me.

"Don't be ashamed to be truthful," I said to the room, then shoved a forkful of the boy's spaghetti into my mouth. "I agree. The pasta is overcooked, and the sauce is bland and way too watery. Not so excellent if you ask me."

While I saw the adults in the room grow tense, I felt the children loosening up around me. They giggled, some even spitting out their food across their brown plastic trays.

"Is this the kind of food you guys want to eat in the middle of your day, after hours and hours of lessons and having to listen to grown-ups who have terrible taste in food tell you what to do?"

There was a collective NO that roared from the children's lips, the false presentation they had been trained to perform all falling away, revealing the pure and perfect children beneath. Still in their prime, at their most honest.

"Tell them. Let them know what you want, what you deserve for all that hard work. All that boring old learning they make us do."

"Grilled cheese!"

"Pizza and french fries!"

"Gummi bears and chicken nuggets!"

I watched as the adults squirmed, each of them falling

into old dishonest habits. Smiling and forcing a laugh toward the children, all a false display to please me. It made me sick, made me realize how much more work we still had to do. Reminded me of the importance of the island. Where we could go the lengths necessary to truly evolve. To reach our individual, unique states of enlightenment.

"Do you hear them?" I asked. I felt more connected with the children in that moment and was grateful for the burst of energy. For the reminder of why my purpose was so crucial. Why I couldn't let anyone, no matter their status or the absurdity of their claims, ever get in the way. My work was imperative—for us all.

Cleft's lip twitched and wiggled as he struggled to hold that fake grin on his face. Keeping his mask in place as he nodded.

"Of course," he said with a hideous wave of his arms. "Tomorrow's menu will have it all … and he's right, children. You absolutely deserve it. Every single one of you—"

"Show me the prison." As I glared into the heart and soul of this disappointing man, I watched as his smile melted from his face like wax in a microwave.

"Yes, Axiom … of course."

I threw a quick sign to Josephine, unable to hold back my smirk. She snorted with laughter and looked the man up and down, sizing him up.

He shrank beneath her judgment before turning and leading us from the cafeteria. The rest of the grown-ups waited for me to follow before trailing behind.

I shot a quick silly face toward the children, crossing my eyes and sticking out my tongue. I rode their laughter through the double doors.

I was eager to see the progress of our corrective measures for those still basking in their lies.

Cleft whispered something to Scar as we strode toward the complex of sheet metal shacks that looked like dog houses at a kill shelter.

Scar nodded but with hesitation, then flashed a smile toward me when she realized I was watching. Clearly being forced to take the lead to allow Cleft to recover from his spat of shame and injured ego.

"These are those who require special attention," she said as she led us between the shacks, giving me a glimpse of the inhabitants. "We're pleased to report that only a third of the shacks are filled. Your acolytes are making real progress here, just as you'd—"

"It seems to me each and every one of these domiciles should be taken," I said, crouching to get a look into the shack beside me. The woman glared back out like a rabid dog in an alley, the corners of her mouth creamed with spit, her lips chapped and bleeding.

"Axiom, we—" Cleft started to say before catching himself and going silent.

"As far as I can tell, the only ones here making any progress are the children. So free of all the lies. Not like you. Not like any of you."

The woman was completely nude and caked in filth. The opposite corner from where she squatted was piled with feces, the brown slop crawling with flies that zipped around the space and suckled her sweaty skin.

Her fingertips bled profusely, dripping from her cracked, sallow nails, which looked chewed down to the quick. Random, chaotic messages were scrawled in sloppy red over the sheet metal walls—

To live in lies is to live in filth.

Over and over and over again. When a red droplet hit her in the cheek, I looked up and saw the ceiling was also written on, the rest of the walls already filled up.

The woman kept her eyes averted, ignoring the dozens and dozens of flies that scuttled across her skin. The floor danced with the writhing of countless maggots, and I could tell from the smell of the woman that she had been in that shack for a week at least.

"Who are you?" I asked her, squatting down to her level

but holding back from touching her.

"I am a liar," she said. "I deserve to wallow in shit with the pests and insects."

I deserve worse than this. I want to be my true self, and I'll do whatever it takes.

I stood and held my hand out to her, no longer concerned with touching the filth of her flesh. It was far less disgusting than the festering lies coating the desperate fools behind me.

"Get up," I said with a smile when her eyes finally coasted toward mine. Stark white orbs floating in the dark grime of her face. "You don't belong here."

"Axiom," she sputtered, the sudden movement of her head as she peered up at me causing the flies to explode into the air and buzz incessantly as they searched for more filth to suckle. "I ... I need to heal and—"

"Your rehabilitation has reached its pinnacle. Now stand and step away from all that waste."

As she took my hand and allowed me to pull her to her feet, I saw another look pass between Cleft and Scar. Cleft then turned to me, his mouth half open as he prepared to dare doubt my decision.

How are we supposed to lead these people if he constantly denigrates and condescends us in front of them?

"Axiom," Cleft started as he stepped toward me, "I think maybe she could use another—"

"No," I interrupted before locking my eyes onto him like daggers through soft bread. "I want you to replace her."

"E-excuse me?"

"I think that somewhere on your journey toward truth, you have lost your way."

I led the woman away from the shit-caked shack toward the tiny rectangular doorway. All but Cleft parted to make room, and as the confused man tried to find support from his peers, he found none. All averted their eyes, refusing to acknowledge him as I continued to berate him.

"I'm sorry you feel that way, Axiom, but I assure you

that I've been nothing but—"

"But what? Honest? True? You can look me in the eye and tell me that for certain?" I released the woman's hand, and she was ushered from the rank domicile by a gentle Josephine, a side of her reserved for specific women—those I assume remind her of herself.

Cleft shifted uncomfortably from foot to foot as I stepped closer and got face to face with him. I searched his eyes for the answer, knowing whatever spilled from his lips next would be basted with falsity.

"I apologize for my failure." His head dropped, chin touching chest. I couldn't see his eyes from that angle but could see his lip twitching once again, just barely able to read his lips. "I only want to please you, Axiom. I only want to serve the ultimate purpose."

"You see, that's the problem." I stepped aside and held my eye contact. After a tense moment, Cleft understood and stepped deeper into the shack. The structure was so short, he had to bend his neck to make room for his head. "My teachings have never been about pleasing me or my purpose. Everyone's journey is their own. Correct?"

I turned to face the other adults standing just outside of the shack, along with the filth-covered woman. They all answered back in unison.

"Yes, Axiom."

"Correct?" I asked again, narrowing my eyes at him.

"Yes, Axiom ... of-of course ..."

"My teachings are about discovering your own truth and living an honest life. And for those that I handpick to join me on this island, to help shepherd the new potential acolytes into our way of living ..." I stepped even closer to him, driving him deeper into the shack, crammed uncomfortably into the corner. His nervous eyes kept darting to the pile of fly-infested feces. I could feel the crunch of the maggots beneath my feet. "I expect more from them. I expect honesty. Not an existence fueled only by the false embrace of another's pleasure."

He nodded, crushing more wriggling larvae into a milky paste beneath his heels. "I understand … I accept that."

I'll be true … anything to make him happy …

I shook my head and sighed, never taking my eyes off him. "*Do* you understand? Show me."

He hesitated a few moments, again looking for support from the others but coming up empty. He nodded again at me, and this time, I could tell he finally understood.

He placed his index finger into his mouth and bit into the tip, cracking the bed of the nail like a plate of glass. Blood welled up instantly and dripped, and without hesitation, he glanced up at the ceiling and found a blank section. Using his blood as ink, he began to write—

—*I will live my truth. I will not live to please others.*

UNDENIABLE TRUTH

The sun had been set for more than an hour, and the presentations were still going. I appreciated their effort and could sense the honesty of their gratitude, but I found myself growing bored and agitated as the tenth performance began.

I had already been subjected to singing and dancing routines, poetry readings, even a magic act. All for me, all so my scarred and disfigured acolytes could welcome me to my island. And though I didn't doubt the truth behind their performances, I couldn't help but see their desperation for my approval. Each one of them competing, even if subconsciously, for my attention. To be my *favorite*.

As the newest trio took the stage and faced me, with all the rest of the island's inhabitants behind me, I glanced toward Josephine. She clearly noticed the frustration and impatience in me because she smirked and quickly signed to me—

"It's almost over. Something very special is coming."

I signed back to her, "Nothing could be more special than all of this ending."

When the trio all swung their guitars from their shoulders and started playing an original song, I clenched my teeth and forced myself to smile and nod my head. A lie, yes, but I didn't want to deter them from displaying their truths—or what they perceived to be their truths, anyway.

I took a moment to glance behind me, toward the dozens and dozens of followers who saw me as their god. Who would follow me to the edge of a cliff and happily dive off into the jagged rocks below if I asked them to.

I was happy to see that Cleft was absent, though I saw Scar clapping along with the music. She had no idea yet that she would be next. Along with the rest of the adults, including the trio singing on stage.

"And now we can feel the lies like an ache in our tooth ... We know that the only thing that matters is to live in our own truth."

This line incited cheers and claps from the audience, the reverberations slithering across my flesh. As my mind started to fill with their thoughts, I quickly closed myself off, disabling my antenna to avoid having to hear their desperate cries for attention.

I glanced back behind me, this time focusing on the children. Each one of them antsy and bored, rolling their eyes rather than pretending to enjoy a song that was as pretentious as it was grating.

I was once again reminded of the purity of the children. Remembered my own childhood, trapped in a home with a woman who wished I never existed. So honest and so innocent. But living a life dedicated to trying to win my mother's love and affection. It was more important than food or shelter—more important than birthday cake.

I realized that adults—including me—had so much to learn from the kids. I wondered how the adults would feel when I told them I was flipping the tables on them. Letting the children call the shots and run the lessons for a bit, teaching each and every one of us what actual unadulterated truth really looks like.

When the song ended, I breathed a sigh of relief, no longer able to keep my little white lie going—that I was at all enjoying this charade.

I glanced toward Josephine to sign another quick joke with her, but I found her seat empty instead. And then I turned to find her standing on the stage.

"Axiom," she said. "You have done so much for all of us. There is something we are eager to share with you. A thank you from your community."

"Oh?" I suddenly felt self-conscious, every pair of eyes on the island now aimed expectantly toward me.

"Would you please join me on stage?" Josephine smiled in a way I hadn't seen in quite some time. And if it would have been anyone else who'd asked, I might have refused. "I think you'll be glad you did, Axiom."

I stood and waved to the crowd, then narrowed my eyes toward Josephine as I signed, "What are you doing?"

"Trust me," she signed back. "This is something special."

I sighed as I gave in and made my way to the stage. When the crowd started to explode into applause, I quickly turned away from them to avoid seeing all those masks of falsity grinning and whistling at me. Kept my eyes glued to Josephine as I climbed the stairs and traipsed across the stage until I reached her.

"We are truly blessed to have you as our leader," she said as she gently grabbed my elbow and turned me until I was forced to face the sea of my acolytes. Every one of them so eager, so enthusiastic for whatever was coming. "Not only did you teach us how to live our truths, but you showed us yours as well. We know exactly who you are."

I watched as she signaled to someone in the distance, someone I couldn't see as the night grew darker by the moment. A projector suddenly clicked to life, blasting a pillar of colorful light toward a lowering white screen.

"No matter what anyone says," Josephine said as the projected image came into focus: a live Zoom chat.

Before I could ask any questions, the line started to ring. I tried to shoot a curious look toward Josephine, but she had her focus on the screen, along with everyone else.

After a few moments, a familiar face filled the screen. A confused expression contorted his countenance.

"Hello?" the man said, his eyes bouncing from left to right as he realized how many faces were looking at him. "What in the hell—who the fuck are you?! How did you get this—?"

"Richard Chapa," Josephine said with a mischievous grin before shooting me an expectant, excited glance—like a child showing their parent a school paper with a thick red A+ etched on the front of it. "You have been spreading lies. Spitting fabrications about our Axiom after everything he did for you. After showing you the light."

Once Richard seemed to realize who he was talking to, his confusion transformed into an equal mixture of anger and satisfaction. Amused that his media tour bad-mouthing the famous Royce O'Riley had gotten under my skin.

"Royce," he said through a toothy smile. "And of course your loyal puppy dragging her ass across the carpet, Josephine. I'd wondered when I'd hear from you."

As I stared up at his smug face, I was filled with a bubbling hatred that was so hot and roiling I knew all of my followers could feel it. The anger momentarily weakened my hold on my talent, a sudden chorus of voices starting to invade my brain. The voices of all my acolytes, roaring and screaming for justice. Begging for vengeance.

I got a hold of it and closed myself off. Not because the voices were assaulting me but because I wanted to be clear as I conversed with Richard. A student who once showed so much promise, so much potential to be truly great and true. He could have been a valuable asset for our great purpose going forward.

But is he not just living his own truth? My own voice echoed through my skull this time. Challenging me, urging me to put my preaching into practice.

Even if that is the case, my conscious mind clapped back, *he has no right to attack me. Me? His savior, his fucking Holy Ghost.*

"Richard," I said, blocking out the rest of the commune. There were no acolytes, no island. Just me and Richard. Eye to eye from thousands of miles away. Yet I could feel the coldness of his stare, hoped he could feel the boiling rage I was psychically sending his way. "I won't waste my time or yours defending myself or accusing you of telling lies for your own financial and social gain."

"Oh, is that right?" He chuckled and shook his head before leaning in closer to his webcam like some giant god staring down at his earthly subjects. "So when I say that you manipulate your subjects to worship you like some kind of fucking messiah, that's a lie? I saw your interview the other night. I, along with millions of other viewers, noticed how you avoided the question about the insemination rituals. I'm not surprised. You are so much about truth, right? You know exactly what you're doing, you sick son of a—"

"The reason we called you this evening," Josephine interrupted, "is to show you that your indiscretions have not gone unnoticed. And will not go unpunished."

Richard laughed, leaning back in his chair and clapping. Really seeming to enjoy himself, so filled with pride for all the harm he'd been attempting to cause.

"Oh, so I'm gonna be punished now, am I? Please tell me what I'm in store for, oh truthful one. I'm in New York, scheduled to be interviewed on the morning show tomorrow. I'll be sure to tell them all about—"

Josephine stuck two fingers into her mouth and whistled. The folks who'd just performed their hearts out for me parted for what appeared to be a trio of figures making their way across the stage.

Once the figures grew closer and the moonlight splashed over them, I recognized the woman ushering the other two forward. A woman with short, natural hair who wore only a crop top so that her recent scars where she'd cut out her own breast implants were visible. Stitched up and pink with healing irritation.

When the woman led the others to my side and I saw the sudden horror erupt across Richard's face, I knew exactly who the middle-aged woman and teenage boy were.

"Linda? Scotty?!" Richard screamed as he stood from his desk so fast he knocked his chair out from behind him to slam into the wall and knock over a collection of hotel framed artwork. "What in the fuck have you …? What are you mother*fuckers* doing with my family?! *Answer me!*"

Josephine took the mother and son away from the flat-chested woman and gave her a subtle nod of dismissal. She nodded and faded in with the others filling the stage.

The rest of the commune were silent—even the children—as they held their breath, waiting to see what I would say or do.

And I wasn't going to make them wait.

"Richard, don't you remember?" I asked before turning away from him and facing his wife and son. Both seemed to be there under their own free will. Both seemed just as disgusted with Richard as I was. "You used to tell me how you'd wanted so desperately to change, to find your truth, for the sake of your wife and son. Both of them were so steeped in lies, you'd said. Both needed my help. Do you remember saying that, Richard?"

"Fuck you, you fucking monster!" I read his shouting lips as foamy spittle flew from them. "Let them go or I swear to God I'll—"

I'm sure he'd continued to shout and threaten me, but I turned toward his family and draped my arms over their shoulders. Pulled them in close, letting my eyes dart from woman to boy and back again.

"Why don't you tell me yourself," I said to them. "Did we force you to be here today?"

The teen boy appeared tentative to answer my question, but the woman seemed to have been waiting her whole life to answer me.

"No," she said, her eyes oozing from my face to the projection of her husband's. "Not at all. In fact, I'd rather be here with all these people than to spend another second in your fucking presence, you prick. I'd rather these strangers raise our son than you. You go on national television, embarrassing us, so you can call out Royce O'Riley for lying? For manipulating? That's fucking rich coming from you. Lying is your language."

I kept my attention on the woman and boy, but I could tell by the facial expressions of the rest on stage, all still watching the projection, that my old friend Richard Chapa was throwing an absolute fit.

"Don't you worry," I told the wife as I took both of her hands in mine, ignoring my revulsion to touch. "I will guide you and your son to the light. I will show you the power of truth. Show you how weak and powerless lies are in the presence of pure honesty."

"Yes," she said, her eyes welling with tears. "Please … please show me. I want to change."

I'll do anything you want … To be free of the lies, I will do absolutely anything …

"And how about you, my son?" I asked the teenage boy, turning my full focus on him as I released his mother's hands and took a firm grip on his shoulders. "What is it that you want in life, hmm? Who are you?"

"I … I, uh … I don't know …"

I just don't want to become my father. I just want my mom to be happy …

"Don't you worry," I said as I squeezed his shoulders to comfort him, leaning my face toward his until he finally locked eyes with me. "If you let me, I'll show you how to be a far better man than your father could have ever hoped to be. And your mother will be so happy to see it happen."

I turned back toward the screen, where Richard was in the middle of a full-on tantrum, his hotel room now trashed as he screamed and hollered.

I just smiled up at him. And winked.

THE LANGUAGE OF LYING

The insemination ritual had begun a few hours earlier than usual. But that night on the island was special, and I was eager for it to get started.

I could tell by the shine on the latex that the strap-ons had been newly molded for this night. None washed and reused from the last ritual. These were freshly pulled from the mold of my own cock. A mold created, with Josephine's help, many years ago. A mold that had been used countless times to create perfect replications of my manhood, each with a reservoir at the tip to be filled with the freshest seed pulled from the most recent milking.

After inadvertently climaxing into Josephine's face, it hadn't taken long for me to finish a second time, which was not common. I typically only had one climax per day available, but my body must have known something truly special was on the horizon. Something that required more seed than usual.

As I watched Richard's wife bend over in front of the short-haired woman with the twin C-section scars beneath her deflated breasts, I felt my loins stir.

The insemination ritual was created when I realized that I had no sexual desires. No appetite for either men or women, yet I had a burning need to procreate. To spread my seed and spawn younger versions of myself, each filled with pure, potent potential to keep my legacy going years and generations after my eventual expiration.

It wasn't enough to have control over my acolytes. It wasn't because my truth wanted me to cause trauma or discomfort for these women. I didn't just want to subject them to these acts for my own enjoyment, watching from behind the glass plate of the two-way mirror.

And because I lacked the sexual desire and was so averse to the physical interaction it would take to sire a child, the insemination ritual was born. I would make a mold of my own cock to create countless copies, each equipped with vinyl straps to secure them to cherry-picked surrogates chosen for their understanding of the importance of this ritual.

I usually chose the new recruits as the wearers, allowing them to fuck my seed into someone who was more of a veteran in my community. Someone who had proven themselves worthy—and biologically able—to carry my child to term. Who would have the capacity to feed and raise them to be strong and sharp.

But this night was different. This night was special.

This night had gifted me with the fertile womb of my enemy. A womb I realized, whether she was a fit mother or not, would be filled with my seed—because my truth wanted it to be so. And I would be damned if I would ignore the desires of my truth.

And so I took great joy as I watched the new breastless acolyte, the one who called herself Rosie, penetrate Mrs. Chapa's cunt with my girthy, short cock, pressing into her slow as she bared her teeth, equal parts pleasure and pressure. I found my own cock hardening and pressing into the zipper of my pants.

Not from sexual excitement. But from the satisfaction of watching Richard Chapa's wife be violated by my member. Watching as her passion grew hotter, her hips rocking, slamming her meaty buttocks into the thrusting groin of Rosie, who gripped the woman's hips with strong fingers. Fucking her with the same eagerness as Josephine had the first time she had been tasked with performing this ritual.

"You see, son?" I whispered into the boy's ear as I held him in place, forcing him to watch as his mother began to scream with ecstasy. "Look how happy she is, hmm? And just think how happy she'll be when she brings your baby brother into the world."

The boy tensed up, trying to pull away from me, back away from the glass. I could see his reflection in the mirror, his mouth opening and closing as if he was trying to say something but couldn't find the words.

But I wouldn't let him go. I held him there so that he had no choice but to witness the truth of his future.

WARM TRUTHS AND BURNING LIES

I stand at the curtain behind the main stage. Feeling the familiar vibrations as the music of my introductory video plays. In this stadium, the largest venue I've ever held one of my seminars, the music echoes over the sold-out crowd.

I'm more excited than usual to see these people. To get out there and open their eyes, their minds to the endless possibilities to find true happiness in their lives.

I wonder how Richard Chapa's interview on the morning show is going. I wonder what he'll think once he finds out what happened with them. When he finds out that I took his wife and son from him.

As the vibrations of the music start to fade, I feel a surge of anticipation build in my gut. Even though I know it's risky and that it's opening me up to vulnerability right before the biggest show I've ever conducted, I open my talent, inviting the thousands of voices waiting for my truth light to blind away all the lies clouding their minds like flailing shadows.

After spending time at the commune, my island of honesty, I realized just how right my decision was to see it through. Even I was doubtful, projecting those doubts onto my loyal acolytes, judging their truths when I was stuck in a moment of uncertainty with my own.

But after what they had done with Richard, gifting me with the clarity of revenge, I know now just how strong my people truly are. And how bright the future looks with the souls of those children.

This stadium is filled with so many potential acolytes to join my cause and help as I spread my influence across the country. Across the world.

My dream is to see the ultimate truth shining down on the Earth like the sun. Washing away all the shadows and darkness with its sharp, burning brightness.

This is the day. The day I change for the better.

Royce O'Riley is the answer. I know he is. I know he'll show me the way!

I'm going to be the very best student. Nobody will be truer than me. I'll show them all!

You lied to me.

I try to zero in on that last thought, closing off my antenna. Blocking the signals flooding my mind from all the others, trying to focus in on whoever it was who'd thought that. Another doubter, a potential threat like Richard.

A tap on my shoulder pulls me out of my mind, making me yelp and flinch as I spin on my heels to face it.

"Are you okay?" Josephine signs to me. "You seem—"

"I'm fine," I say back, using my voice. "This show means everything. Can't you feel it? There's something powerful out there. Just waiting for me. And I won't make it wait, not a second longer."

When I say this to her, I see something come over her. A change in her expression. I can't pinpoint what it is, as if she just remembered some traumatic suppressed memory. Whatever it is that's running through her brain is so potent that she doesn't even respond to me.

I narrow my eyes at her, locking my stare to see if she'll snap out of it and stop disrespecting me. It's not like Josephine, and I make a mental note to address this moment later with her. Remind her that I expect far more from my number two than I do anyone else on the island.

I leave her behind and step past the curtain and onto the stage. As the crowd explodes into uproarious applause, I have to focus harder than ever to close my mind to them. I can feel the hurricane of their thoughts ripping into my skull, desperate to spray their message across my brain.

You lie to everyone.

This time, when the words ooze into my mind, there's a heat to it. As if the slow cooker of my head was just turned on, slowly roasting my brain.

But I ignore it as I smile and wave to my people. Their love and adoration is so loud I can feel the vibrations of their cries and claps.

"Ladies and gentlemen!" I cry, my arms stretched out to my full wingspan. I have to fight to keep my smile on my face as I pace the front of the stage and allow the audience to appreciate my presence before them. "Wh-who's ready to rise ... rise above all the ..."

You lie to yourself.

I'm unable to ignore the pain this time, dropping the microphone as the heat in my skull intensifies and it feels like my brain is ballooning and expanding, trying to break free from the bone.

I turn to find Josephine, to signal to her that something isn't right. That I need her now more than ever before.

But her expression is full of panic and pain. Her eyes bloodshot and crying crimson rivers that paint crooked lines down her quivering cheeks.

She reaches her hands out to me as if to sign something. Some silent cry for help that only I would understand. Our own language, just the two of us.

But before she has a chance to form a single word with her fingers, both of her eyes pop like grapes, spraying twin spurts of blood from her empty eye sockets.

And then the rest of her head erupts. A shower of gore and skull fragments blast from the top of her neck, leaving behind a jagged stump that fountains blood as the body goes limp and collapses to the floor.

And then, from behind me, exploding from somewhere in the audience. Like a bazooka blast inside of my head.

Look at me.

The pain drops me to my knees, my skull now a pressure cooker cranked up to its highest temperature. I watch as the faces of the crowd become masks of confusion and panic, watching as my brain is cooked in front of them.

And then I see her. One special face amongst the crowd. Like a tiny island of the most truest truth I'd ever felt before. Truer than my own, than the children, than my mother's.

Her eyes are locked onto me as a sinister grin stretches her mouth as wide as it will go.

Look into my eyes and tell me the truth.

Look into my eyes and honestly tell me that you are not a liar.

The pressure keeps building, the heat intensifying. I can feel the blood boiling and seeping from my orifices.

Hotter and hotter, fuller and fuller.

Everything goes red. Everything but this woman's face.

And then—

—darkness. Pure and peaceful darkness.

Forever and ever.

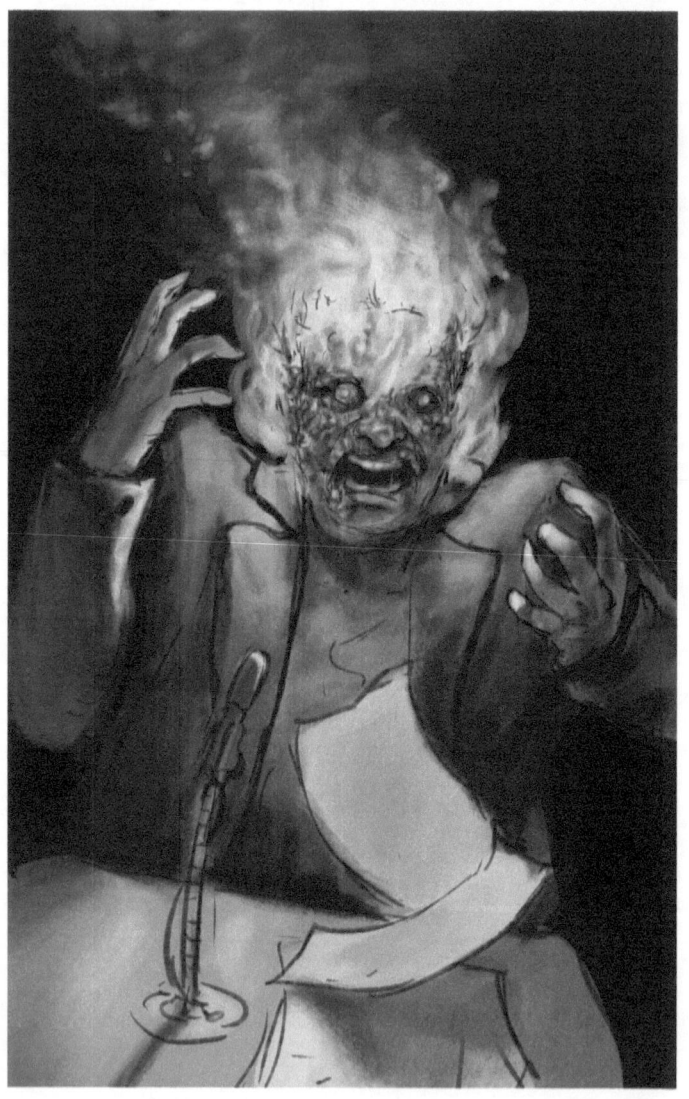

ABOUT THE AUTHOR

Aron Beauregard just recently turned 21. Despite several conflicting reports, silver hair, a bum ankle, and a toe that cracks every time he takes a goddamn step, he's ONLY 21— definitely *not* 40. Now that he is of legal drinking age, he will no longer partake. Mostly because it's not fun to do stuff that's legal. He's planning on maybe going to college and getting learnt up. But more than likely, he feels that he may tool around for a decade or so before writing some books that will cause mainstream society to banish him forever.

ABOUT THE AUTHOR

John Skipp is a horror legend, splatterpunk founding father, and New York Times bestselling author-turned-filmmaker whose books have sold millions of copies worldwide, and also on other planets. His most recent feature film is THE GREAT DIVIDE, and his scrotum is a conjoined twin named Leopold who whimpers in the night, but speaks Polish fluently.

ABOUT THE AUTHOR

Shane McKenzie tells everyone that he's Korean and Scottish, but that is a lie. His Scottish father and Korean mother stole him off the streets of Mexico in the early 80s and gave him a name they thought would fool the world and lead to his great success which they hoped to profit off of. His real name is Consuelo Santiago De La Cruz and he has written many books and comics including *Benjamin* with Aron Beauregard and *Monsters Don't Cry*, as well as films such as Blumhouse's *Bingo Hell* and the biopic *Jenni*. His parents are extremely disappointed and are planning another trip to Mexico soon.

Talk about a filmmaker who bleeds for his art!

Nightmare legend John Skipp was one of the original splatterpunks, pioneering a fresh style of literary horror that was smart, savage, sexy, cinematic, unbelievably gory, wickedly subversive, and fiercely fun.

Now writer-turned-filmmaker Skipp presents his new movie THIS IS SPLATTERPUNK: a wild, definitive statement on horror's rowdiest, most rebellious subgenre.

By showing, not telling, Skipp's provocative feature drops FOUR INSANE SHORT FILMS that illustrate the difference between original 80's **splatterpunk**, the **traditional horror** it slammed up against, and the two types that spun off from it when it died: **Extreme horror** and **Bizarro**.

Part deranged anthology film, part educational personal statement, and 100% designed to kick ass, THIS IS SPLATTERPUNK is landmark horror about landmark horror. You have never seen anything like it.

To learn more about THIS IS SPLATTERPUNK and how to support, scan the QR code below.

COMING SUMMER OF 2025!

EVERY PLAYGROUND HAS A PROTOTYPE

Geraldine Borden has realized that there's one thing her bottomless wealth can't grant her: children. When an attempt to remedy her infertility fails, she's left with nothing but rage, jealousy, and a murderous idea. She aims to take a place that all children adore and transform it into a twisted arena of carnage. And while her true masterpiece is still under construction, she seeks to entertain herself with a crude prototype filled with barbaric backyard games.

Several children from a small New England city have gone missing under mysterious circumstances. This group of kids— who once believed fractured family and teen angst were their toughest battles—now have a whole new set of problems. With no parents to guide them, will the children thrust into Geraldine's nightmare world have the grit and determination to escape? Or will they fall victim to their sadistic captor?

The much-anticipated prequel to Aron Beauregard's controversial book *Playground* revisits some of the author's most reprehensible characters. It includes 18 interior illustrations and pushes the limits of incendiary literature even further.

WARNING: This book contains graphic content. Reader discretion is advised.

AVAILABLE NOW!

NATASHA JUST WANTS TO BE LOVED

But it's hard to find someone when you're a hideous, disfigured monstrosity of a human.

She knows she'll never be beautiful like the women in the magazines, but the porcelain doll mask she wears helps her feel pretty.

She has spent her life locked in her bedroom by her bitter, abusive mother. But one day, fate provides an opportunity and Natasha finds herself free to explore the outside world.

She wants to find love - no matter how many crushed skulls or disembowelments it takes. She will find her Prince Charming, even if she has to rip the world apart.

WARNING: This book contains graphic content. Reader discretion is advised.

FOR SIGNED BOOKS, MERCH, AND
EXCLUSIVE ITEMS FROM ARON BEAUREGARD VISIT:

ABHORROR.COM

FOR SIGNED BOOKS, MERCH, AND
EXCLUSIVE ITEMS FROM SHANE MCKENZIE VISIT:

McHORROR.NET